I0586189

A High Country Romance

MARGOT LA FONTAINE

A High Country Romance

Thank you very much for your
help in producing this novel:
Rachel Sirr , Louise Molony,
Amanda Proos, Wendy Wilson
and David Potter

One

'Hang dang it! Blinkin heck that hurt! Owww!'

Alice sat on the ground rocking back and forth clutching her throbbing little toe. Angry at herself, the pain enraged her as she sat, alone in her terrace house. Alone, apart from her cat of course. She had (yet again), whacked her toe against the foot of her old couch.

Tabby the cat curled and entwined himself around her back purring comfortingly. 'Tabby,' sighed Alice, stroking the cat's vibrating throat. 'What good is it? I can't even find my way around my own flat, and it's only the size of a postage stamp. Why don't I just stay here with you for the rest of my life?'

The cat answered with a deep rumble from the depths of its furry belly, and rolled over for a tummy rub, some drool began to collect at the side of his lip.

She bowed her head in despair feeling her face wet and slimy with tears. She cuddled the cat tighter, and with this the cat struggled to get free. She went to get up and tripped over him.

'Ooh!' she screamed, her temper flaring up again. 'Stupid cat! Get out of my way!' The cat fled, but as soon as she sat on the couch, he was back and hopped up onto her knee.

It was another night to trip over things.

'How many times do I have to crack my toe into the leg of the couch? I guess I'll keep doing it until I learn. Even a single cell amoeba manages to avoid something in its path after a while!'

Night times seemed to last forever and when morning came, she struggled with her depression. In her dreams she would be in a Stephen's warm embrace, and now she instead she would wake to find a cat curled on her chest steadily purring. This was just where he liked to sleep like a great growth on her chest soaking up all her warmth but also transmitting his own.

Her small townhouse faced the railway line. Yep, enough to wake you up every few minutes at night. Just getting out of bed seemed impossible, especially when cold frost held her small flat in its grip. Waking and sleeping all blended together with relentless certainty leaving her afraid of the future. Could she keep up with ordinary routines like eating, shopping for food and remaining clean and well dressed? A few years back she floated through life on a perpetual high. Now, she barely coped and often felt close to the precipice of insanity. She would wake, dress, go to the Rehabilitation Centre, work and then come home. The next day would follow in much the same way.

It was a far cry from the uptown, stylishly attired woman that she had been. Then, she would always wear the latest and the greatest. 'Yep', she sighed, 'I had it all and I had you, you, *you!*'

Her radio alarm clock woke her in the morning, as usual playing pathetic rock FM. It was a song about Pina colada sand dunes and romance which made her want to give it a good smashing. 'How cruel oh sleep,' she muttered out loud, 'deny the love its lover, the dove its mate, morning is here much too late.' She often did that, wake up speaking poetry. It definitely gave her a small thrill of enjoyment, amidst her usual depression. She was exhausted from clenching every muscle in her sleep, and she slumped out of bed.

Alice stumbled into the shower; eyes half closed. 'When you died Stephen, you might as well have killed me.' she said out loud. Water ran down her face. She scrubbed her pale, almost luminescent skin, trying to almost rub herself away. *You and I were mates, I was as much a bloke as you – and we were soul mates…cliché I know. Yes, we were mates even though I didn't drink beer but I'd drink one with you now if only you were here. I'd wear a navy-blue singlet and watch the football with you! Our pizza nights are gone forever. How could you leave me? I need you. You were the one and now without you, I feel like I'm slowly dying too.* She got out, and roughly towel dried her hair, which was cut into a shoulder length choppy do. She wouldn't have time to style it this morning. It used to be blonde, long, sleek, and all one length with a few helpful highlights, People would admire it. But was now was chopped to a sensible manageable length, and gone were her days of colouring. She had gone all natural – in fact she couldn't even remember what that was. It had turned darker almost grey-brown ash blonde. Despite the dull colour, and the somewhat frumpy cut, it was still thick and shiny. She faced the bathroom mirror. *I'm sure I look ugly and hideous – how would I know? I've really let myself go. I used to feel like a princess when Stephen looked at me. Now I think frumpy thoughts so that's probably what I look like – frumpy.*

'Where is my jumper, the hairy one? I think I put it over on the back of the chair away from the cat…Oh no! Tabby, you filthy beast get off it.' The jumper had slipped onto the seat of the chair and was undoubtedly covered in hair. Alice face burnt and then her eyes stung. She was coming to the boil and if Tabby knew what was good for him, he would get the heck out of there.

'Breathe in goodness, out tension, in goodness out tension. Mmmmmm I can feel it!' She felt sorry for herself but she was also angry. An uncharitable thought crossed her mind about the cat. She could simmer quite a while but eventually she would come to the boil and then blow. *I'm like Vesuvius. I thought crying was meant to release stress but I cry and explode as well. A highly volatile concoction and I get a thumper of a headache! It's hardly worth it.* He dropped fur everywhere and especially on her good dark clothing (or so she was told by well-meaning people at the Rehabilitation centre). Now he was dripping saliva on her clothes, something he did when he was in a really good mood, cat ecstasy actually. She would have gladly tossed him out of the window but she knew it wasn't far enough to cause him injury.

Cats can really get on your nerves with their need to be constantly fed. She had time for memories, and while she was angry with the cat, she was not focusing on her fiancée's absence…but she still remembered it nearly every waking hour and also while she was asleep. She knew she was obsessed and probably needed counselling but was too proud and was enjoying (in a sick way) her sad reveries.

She had time to spoon in a few mouthfuls of low-fat muesli. It was surprisingly tasty but she felt she had done a day's work already just chewing it up. She found the box of cereal, poured herself a portion followed by some milk, and sat at the kitchen table munching, half listening to the TV in the background.

They keep telling us on the telly that having a pet is so good for you. Lowering your blood pressure? What a joke! Tabby makes mine skyrocket – or I think he does anyway! They say that patting an animal lowers your blood pressure (and it probably does). It's the other things that make it skyrocket, like feeding and grooming it. A long-haired cat is hell to groom and they knot up overnight. Taking it to the vet to get its teeth descaled or some other expensive procedure is all going to put blood pressure up, to say nothing of the risk of mauling and or severe puncture wounds by worming it. And worming? Cats seem to develop twenty or so arms and a full barrage of bristling barbs the moment you try to open their mouths to worm them. And of course, let's not forget cleaning up its poo.

The cat was the scapegoat for her anger and grief. She couldn't forget the real pain there in the back of her mind always. How well she remembered the police helicopter's loud choppers. Lights, voices…a stretcher borne down the slope.

'Who was in that stretcher Alice?' she asked herself cruelly.

She winced as the pain reached deep into her again. She closed her eyes to try to escape. It made no difference. Everything was cloaked in velvety black darkness. *I knew damn well who it was! It had to be him! I knew it in the pit of my stomach the moment*

I saw the stretcher.

She let out a dry sob, struggled with her breath for a moment, and then swallowed. She needed to keep munching her tasteless cereal or she would be late. After brushing she had to carefully floss to make sure a stray oat didn't lodge in a prominent position to spoil her dazzling smile. Of course, oats got stuck in the front teeth. Even if Jacquie told her it was there, she was humiliated and knew that everyone else had seen it. *I don't plan on smiling much today anyway.* She hoped none had fallen onto her clothes.

Ten went abseiling that day and I wasn't one of them, because I'm scared of heights. Such a coward, and if I came it would have been eleven people, an odd number. I should have gone as well. I should have gone! Why couldn't it have been someone else? she thought feeling her bitterness rise up like poison. *Yes, why not someone else? We were going to be married.* Tears came now, and dripped from her nose into her mouth and into her cereal, and the cat gave a yowl as it demanded more food. She rose, grabbed Tabby and flung him out of the front door, sighing with fierce relief but feeling a bit guilty as well. 'Cats always land on their feet' she sniffed as she took her bowl to the sink. But she knew that taking her anger out on an innocent animal was pretty weak behaviour, and she immediately felt remorse.

'Tabby, Tabby?' she opened the door and called out. *How could I treat my best friend this way? I hope he's alright.* Her heart beat powerfully in her chest and she started to feel sick.

I hope I haven't hurt him! Just sabotaging another loved one,

12

that's me!

Sardonically, through her tears she thought of the old saying that she had just proven true. Her place *was* 'big enough to swing a cat in.'

She heard a few splatters rain begin to patter against the window. 'Great.' She thought. Now I have to hold an umbrella and a cane. In the rain.' despite herself, she smiled wryly at her pathetic pun.

If only Stephen was still here – he'd know what to do. He had selfishly – she decided – done his daring exploit. If only he had stayed on firm ground, instead of the stupid abseiling adventure.

That last day we could have been together just one more time just doing stuff together like dyeing his hair, yes even dying (of the very permanent kind) together wouldn't have been so bad! Her emotional excess, dropped, splashed but they couldn't wash away the ache in her chest.

She picked up one of Stephen's jumpers off the couch that still smelt of him and she hadn't washed it. 'I need you to cuddle me, I need you so much! I'll probably never cuddle another man, just a stupid cat and it's probably run away from home!' The mantelpiece clock chimed seven times and the image of Stephen's sandy hair and cheeky grin, a wild spirit, disappeared into the city driven away by pelting rain. She felt a fluffy thing curling around her legs. He had come through the cat flap which she had left open hoping he would return. It was good timing because she had to leave. 'You are such a disappointment Tabby. I wish you were him but you're just a dumb animal, dumber than most.' Tabby couldn't care less. He had forgiven her for hurling him outside into the rain.

As she locked up her townhouse and put up her Monet-pictured umbrella, and a fresh wave of sadness swept over her. She pulled out her cane and tapped to the bus-stop. 'God,' she whispered, *'I can only take so much of life without love. I need you and I don't want any more pain. You know you have my attention but I'm just too weak and sad to leap guts and all into life. Please care for me. I know I am meant to be happy or to have recovered by now but I don't want to listen to people telling me not to be so selfish, to get over it, to build a bridge and get over it. I hate those bastards* she thought furiously. There was a time when pat answers from my well-meaning friends would have been enough. Well known platitudes such as: 'God has a reason for this. Good will come out of this. The pain is a good discipline. It strengthens character. *Oh yes, such comforting words for those in the black hole. It's so great to think that I will have a better character now that I've lost my fiancée and am blind. Maybe I should have turned really bad and still have fiancée and sight. God, you know I'm pretty far gone but honestly if one more person tells me to buck up, I may deck them.*

I just want to talk to you because I don't trust the rest especially all of those quick fix people.

She nearly lost a shoulder rushing through the front door of the bus.

'How are you going Al?' said Joe the bus driver giving her a hand up.

'Just great Joe, I'm jumping out of my skin can't you tell?' said Alice. 'I'm sick of tap cane dancing. Do you think I would be as good as Ginger Rogers in all those ancient Fred Astaire dance movies? This is quite a crowd pleaser don't you think?' she tapped her stick around madly and gave a gloomy hop. Suddenly she tripped up the bus steps.

'Steady on old girl!' Joe grabbed her arm just in time.

Gaining her composure, she giggled with embarrassment.

'Yep, I'm an old girl now, am I? Thanks for that. Really does a lot for the ego. Was I good?'

'The tap cane dance?' Joe grimaced. 'Oh, very professional!' Joe eased the bus away from the curb and continued driving the route.

Alice sat in the front near the driver and kept up the conversation as he drove.

Joe kept up the banter. 'You could go somewhere with that. All you need to make it pay is a black Labrador with soulful eyes and a hat. By the way there's a huge something in your front teeth.'

'I could blind you with my stick for that. Thank you! The whole bus heard about my dental hygiene! You're quite adroit at dealing with this indelicate subject and my personal feeling in relation to it.' laughed Alice despite herself.

'OK honey, I don't even know what that means!' exclaimed Joe.

Alice sighed, then said 'It means you're a bit tactless.'

Joe shook his head and trying not to grin broadly, as Alice discreetly picked at her teeth behind her tissue.

'And *by the way*', asked Alice with sarcasm tingeing her voice, 'Is that huge something gone from my teeth?'

'It's gone. You're miss grumpy today! I might have to put you in the baggage cage so you can't savage anyone.'

Alice gave Joe a withering look 'So you think I have excess baggage?' exclaimed Alice haughtily.

'Who doesn't?' said Joe reefing the wheel around a corner after stopping at another stop and lurched on its way. Her stop was next.

She shook her head and smiled. Joe grinned and gave her a cocky salute and said, 'Just try to keep those claws in today, OK?'

'I can't promise anything.' said Alice with a toss of her head as she tapped toward the bus doors.

'Hey!' exclaimed Joe reeling back in mock fear. 'You should be on the endangered list, a Tasmanian Tiger.'

'No, no, no! That's a marsupial and it doesn't claw anyone and I'm not Tasmanian!' corrected Alice.

'Of course. You win. Gotta go now. Try to be good and…'

'Yes, I know, and if I can't be good then be good at it. It makes me bored even finishing your sentence, Joe.'

The bus driver added with a grin, 'Well be bad then, and enjoy it!' With that he swung the wheel turning the vehicle into the main stream of traffic. Alice smelt the damp Melbourne air mixed with vehicle fumes. It smelt grey, she thought. She felt herself slump as she contemplated being at work for the rest of the day. Having fun with the bus driver at least made her feel alive. How she longed for the old days when she had fun all the time. And then there was shopping, a truly desirable pastime. What could she admire now in those glossy windows?

She walked to her work only a matter of a hundred metres or so.

Alice sat and typed on the Braille type writer most of the day, making new books for the library and made various 'things' which seemed to be composed mainly of glue. The Rehabilitation Centre had been a vital place for her in the months after Steven's death – after she lost her eyesight. She had been grateful for their help in learning to function, learning to read and later type Braille. Now that they had offered her a parttime job, she was even more grateful.

She didn't want to be accused of wallowing in deep self-pity so she went through the motions 'helping herself', but deep down she ached, she wept and felt violated. To be expected to be cheerful infuriated her, as all she wanted to do was cry. *One day I'm going to be clean out of tears. That'll be the day! Crying has nothing to show for it but exhaustion and pain the same as dry retching does. Why do I have to be in so much agony, all the time! I think I've reached the point where I enjoy it. At least I feel something even if it is unbearable.*

She remembered the well-known apt but depressing little saying: 'Laugh and the world laughs with you, cry and you cry alone.' *Well, that would ambush any real communication since people only want to have anything to do with you when you are happy, happy, happy! When they say 'and how are you today, Alice?' I can't actually tell them can I because they don't really want to know. They can't handle the truth so there's no honesty. It's all rubbish.*

In a way she wished she didn't have any friends at all because she felt guilty around them. Perhaps a lethal dose of dopamine would give her a high and her friends could admire her cheeriness before she died. They didn't have to be in her zone. She was stuck in that zone now and apart from brief moments of happiness that was where she stayed.

At lunchtime she munched through her sandwich alone. Many times, the others had invited her to sit with them but she usually politely declined. Now they couldn't be bothered asking her any more. She listened to their loud chatter, banter and occasional tearing to pieces some poor individual who was not present. It really made lunch time nasty. Even on the occasion that she did join them she tended to drift into a kind of morose isolation that froze others off. By this time of the day, she was almost spent and she could have had an early mark but didn't because that would be admitting weakness and unreliability as an employee. *Heck they are probably going to talk about me now that I'm over here and out of earshot. I need company that's the thing. I need company but then when I've got it, I don't want it – like the cat. Darn it would be good to stroke him now. He'll probably be a bit wary tonight after the hurling incident.*

What the egg-flip do I care anyway. They can rip into me if they like. I'd kind of like it. It's become enjoyable in a weird way. Wallowing in misery, yes, that's it and yes, it's sort of nice, like the sad music I listen to these days. Damn I think I need a dose of high-octane Disco Inferno. I love that song! There's something so sexy, so alive and powerful about it. Janne, danced to the Disco Inferno during her contractions while she was giving birth. I need a bit of distraction. A bit of life but I don't actually want to give birth – but then again yes, I do but it's too late. Her heart shrank as she thought about the child she would never have. She was on quite a roll, being depressed about several things at once. Was that or perhaps it was multiple melancholy multitasking.

'Hey Alice!' called Jacquie cheerily manoeuvring her wheel chair skilfully next to Alice.

'Yes, Jacquie?' answered Alice, listlessly but marvelling at Jacquie's propensity for always being up.

'I'm having a party this Saturday at about six thirty. Want to come? It'll be fun. Funky fun. You can bring your old disco C.D. and you know what that means…'

Both together said with sheer exhilaration: 'Disco Inferno!'

'You know I was just thinking about that! Do you think I'm psychic?' mumbled Alice.

'Maybe.' A short silence, 'But now tell me – do you want to come?' 'I may be busy.'

'Yeah, yeah, busy, *busy*! Right! Clipping your cats toe nails, and after that you have to sweep them up!' That'll be fun! Come on, it can't do you harm. You might even meet a nice bloke if indeed that mythical creature exists!'

'Might? Right!' Alice scowled. 'I can assure you he did exist and I loved him. And like the last of the Mohican Indians, he was the one and only last one on earth. Nice men are extinct.,' said Alice coldly, before she could even censor the grumpiness of her comment and make it suitable for general exhibition.

'Yes, I know. You can say I'm being insensitive,' continued Jacquie 'but it's nearly eight years honey…' Alice looked down, knowing what was coming next. 'We've talked about this before. Don't you think Stephen would like you to get a move on?'

'How would I know what he wants?' Alice said loudly. A few people glanced over, but then went back to their chatter. 'He is probably totally happy in heaven and doesn't need a reminder of his boring mortal girlfriend. I can't give him up just yet.'

Jacquie sighed. 'Look.

Alice led on to a little whine. 'I didn't know there was a time limit on grief! It would take a pretty amazing and mythical male to want to be with a blind girl…a miserable one at that. When should I be over Stephen, Jacquie? Today? tomorrow?'

'Alice, you're very darn dramatic.' said Jacquie.

'It's all very well to tease about it but it's my loss not yours and I still feel he is the only man I will ever bond to – you know bond as in soul mate bonding. If you don't like me being like this just roll on by and don't talk to me. By the way I had a friend who was divorced and it took her a good six years to get over that! She cried every night for six months! It's normal to grieve over a great loss and I think I am being reasonable.' Alice folded her arms stuck her nose in the air.

'Now, now.' Jacquie put her arm around Alice and patted her on the head as if she were a small pup. Alice stiffened and folded her arms defensively.

Jacquie continued. 'You know I'm quite shallow but I've never had a grand love affair the way you did. All I know is it would do you good to get out and about a bit. Your closest companion is that cat. True?'

'Yeh.' groaned Alice, 'and he's not even got a pedigree!' How could I spend so much time and effort on such a tacky tabby?' She swiftly turned her face away. 'And he's probably even run away by now 'cause I threw him across the kitchen and I don't even remember what he was doing wrong.'

'Was he was nagging you for food?' asked Jacquie knowingly.

'How did you know that?'

'Cats only sleep, hunt or beg for food and they don't hunt if they don't have to. It wasn't hard to guess.'

Jacquie tried again – 'Now this party will be super *fun*! I've invited alternative people as opposed to city stereotypes you know, sensible people. There are a few intellectuals for you.'

'What do you mean exactly by alternative people? Alternative to what? canines, bovines, supines, equines, rodenta, crustacea, porifora, nematoda?' snapped Alice the corner of her mouth twitched as she held back a smirk and the start of a delicious tickling giggle.

'You just proved you're an intellectual just then – with that zoological jargon.' said Jacquie somewhat shocked and impressed by Alice's knowledge about what she thought sounded like Latin terminology of the animal kingdom.

'I'm just sensitive and humble like you!' said Alice. A chuckle surprised her, rising suddenly from the pit of her stomach. Her soft drink bubbled out of her nose causing her to laugh even more.

Jacquie shrieked: 'You are *so* embarrassing!' 'You can't handle your drink and you speak Latin; I'm leaving! I thought that the only Latin I would ever have to hear was at my old Catholic School!'

Alice was still laughing and mopping up the froth coming out of her nose and giggled 'Don't you want me to tell you about echinodermata and platyhelminths?'

'Not really.' said Jacquie looking around the cafeteria uncomfortably.

There was a loud hissing splutter as the cafeteria cappuccino machine created coffee.

More froth.

'Well?' inquired Jacqueline hopefully, still there waiting while Alice pulled herself together. 'What do you think about the party – and please don't use any more scientific terms on me either. I couldn't stand it'.

She couldn't speak above the sound of the cappuccino machine. It stopped and the two women faced each other across the cafeteria table.

Jacquie studied her friends face, realizing that in fact, they had now known each other for six years, and Alice quite possibly was her best friend. She met her two years after the accident, and Alice had been a broken girl of only 22. Now, Jacquie saw strength in her friend's face – she was stronger, and had found accomplishment in learning how to read and write Braille, and had become a skilled facilitator at the Rehabilitation centre. And Jacquie thought, Alice hadn't really changed in looks – even at 28, she looked better now than when they first met at 22, Jacquie thought that it was time for her to meet someone. To move on from Stephen. It was easier or Jacquie to think that though, having never known Stephen. To Jacquie, he was just a memory that belonged to Alice's past, and a memory that was holding Alice back from the rest of her life.

'I think, I think' said Alice with fingers to her temple s divining some feedback from her intuition. 'I think …yeh, why not.' I don't want to be a killjoy and it is really nice for you to invite me, a renowned depressive to come to your party. Jacquie laughed and slapped Alice lightly across the head, messing up her hair. She sped away in her wheel chair. 'Mission accomplished!' she giggled.

Two

The day of the party came and Alice climbed out of the taxi to have her senses accosted by the loud laughter of many people and the rhythmic, stereo bass playing trendy coffee-house jazz, and constantly clinking glasses. She was glad she didn't have a seeing-eye dog. *They are such an attraction and everyone loves to befriend a seeing-eye dog but it would put me in the lime light and I definitely don't want that!* Alice was thinking that a seeing-eye cat would have suited her as a more secretive creature that would curl up somewhere quiet when surrounded by pandemonium or just clear out.

I could have accompanied it into the drawer of a desk – a big desk of course, maybe a tall boy. Tabby didn't like it the last time I trapped him in the drawer of my tall boy at home. Oh yes, he kept yowling till I found him. Kerrie's kitten got spun dry. It didn't survive. My God Alice get a grip! Stop rambling to yourself! Live for the moment for once in your life!

Jacquie's many friends knew her from before her diving accident. She was to them the same old Jacquie but Alice knew differently. Jacquie was just good at putting on a good front and a good show for that matter. She missed like heck the fact that she would no longer run along a windy beach, that she could no longer saunter around the markets at the same height as the general public.

She was a little lower some would say than the angels. It was a bit like being a dwarf, viewing people from the waist up. Not an empowering position. Her friends loved her still and had not only stuck by her but flocked around her. She seemed to attract people and always had several hovering about her like bees around a can of soft drink. Jacquie left her friends and came over to see how her nervous friend was faring.

'Hey!! You made it! How are you doing? What can I get you to drink?'

'Oh, good, I'm good, *really!*' said Alice.

Jacquie spun around a grabbed her a glass of champagne from a tray and shoved it into her hands.

She held the stem of the glass for dear life. It was a comfort to have something to hold. Jacquie kept her voice low 'Most of the people here are sporty, from trail riding, netball, tennis, whatever, you name it. I never (or rather let me rephrase that) I never got many blue ribbons but I did have a go and I'm really glad I gave it all a go. It's all been fun.

Her voice trailed off wistfully.

Then she perked up. 'Just wait till the next Paralympics! I'll kill'm! Man, my arms have built up from this wheel chair! Just look at these guns – oh sorry I forgot you can't see them.' With that she said, 'Come on, I'll introduce you to some people if you like.'

'No' gasped Alice smoothing her hair down. 'I *don't* like! Unlike you I don't have a myriad of sports to talk about and I gather that this party is mainly for the lycra set and I have a serious aversion to lycra.'

'Now, now!' laughed Jacquie, that sounds a trifle uncharitable and just for your information I did invite some nerds, couple of computer egg heads but they had the Star Wars convention tonight. One of them does that asthmatic Darth Vader breathing thing really realistically!'

'Thanks Jacquie but I would rather join my cat in the dryer, or the top drawer of the tall boy.' There was a brief pause, before Jacquie said slyly, 'There are other types of tall boy,' 'Not interested!' Alice gritted her teeth at the thought meeting a new man who wasn't Stephen.

'If you're trying to kill yourself, why go to the trouble of torturing yourself. Either you want to live to enjoy the torture or you want to cop out and die quickly. I suppose the clothes dryer would be the best it would torture you a fair bit before you died, pretty cramped, though. Look, just stop it! Stop it! *Stop it!* We are having this morbid little conversation *again!*' Jacquie scanned the room to check on her guests. The party was really happening with people mingling, talking loudly.

'I know we are only joking but…Hell Alice, how about getting smashed?' she smiled goofily. 'I know you probably don't approve of it – being a Christian – but a little alcohol would probably help you relax and stop thinking of ways to do yourself in. Jeez! Now you've got *me* talking a lot of crap! Jacquie was exasperated. 'Just be a good girl and put on a happy face. She patted Alice's hand like an old Auntie. 'They may even think you're normal!'

'Ouch! Jacquie that was a bit mean! I accept my admonishment'

'Enjoy it and remember not all of us carry dictionaries!' said Jacquie.

'I promise to behave!'

'If you don't you will have to sit on the naughty chair, but knowing you, you'll probably like it!' said Jacquie sounding like a school teacher. 'You know, all that shame and punishment! I can hear you drooling from here.' Alice smiled sardonically. Jacquie gulped down the last of her second glass of wine. 'Come on Alice! Mingle, mingle! You mustn't remain single!'

'OK, OK. It will be painful…but it'll be a good kind of pain!' laughed Alice wanting to please her friend who really was her bestie these days.

Jacquie looked sceptical 'Sure Alice, I know you. You'll sneak away somewhere and reappear when it's a socially acceptable time to go home.'

Alice smiled. 'Look I really promise I'll make an effort once I've had some fresh air, OK? And, by the way if all your friends are so health conscious why are they smoking out the place?'

'Mmmmm we'll see.' was all Jacquie replied. 'I'll be checking up on you.' With that she wheeled away leaving Alice to herself which was what Alice thought she wanted, but wistfulness set in and she tried to fade into the background. Just because she couldn't see them didn't mean they didn't see her.

She grabbed a piece of hair and twirled it vigorously. Then she started biting her lower lip. Time to escape. She felt like a nobody special with nothing to say that anyone would want to hear. It wasn't just bloody-minded reclusiveness but a complete lack of self-esteem that caused her to run away from others.

How could she captivate anyone, let alone these accomplished athletic stars? What could she say? *I walk two hundred yards to the bus stop every day. I have a cat which, I haven't spun dry yet but I've been tempted to. Sometimes I wake up in the middle of the night and write four-line poems. I am still mourning my fiancée who eight years ago died on a cliff without me, when I could have accompanied him which would have been a blessing compared to the way I feel now. Oh, yes and I am blind.* No, retreat was the only option. She wanted to get away before she infected someone with her depressing tale.

Alice ran her hand along the edge of the lounge and then lightly past the wall units. There was the arch of the lounge door way. She was doing well not having run into anyone yet.

Hooooorah! she thought. *Freedom is almost mine! I'm nearly at the front door yes here I'm on the verandah!*

The humid summer air enveloped her face, fragrant, with the smell of the grass which, was a little damp from the sprinkler. She sighed as a couple of small tears formed in her eyes, and her throat thickened with many more threatening to fall. This smell in the air reminded her of carefree afternoons she had spent in Stephen's parent's back yard. It was nothing momentous, just barbeques, swimming and cricket with his brothers. It was funny, no downright strange, how circumstances, places and people and your very nature could be cruelly sabotaged by life. Still, it was nice to get some fresh air into her lungs so she just stood with her hands on the rail of the verandah and missed the past, much as she wanted to enter into the present and even – dare she contemplate it – the future!

'Ah, sweet summer,' she sighed out loud. She was proud of her not too noticeable exit from the smoky room filled with jabbering people. Yes, this was what she loved best. To be alone on a hot summer's evening, breathing the bouquet that nature gave. Simple things like water and grass.

Her own little flat in the city was devoid of greenery except for a few water-starved pot plants. Jacquie was fortunate to live here in blessed suburbia in the little island of lushness and chlorophyll bursting from every stoma. Or whatever chlorophyll did.

Chlorophyll and greenness were doing her good and possibly the stomata were as well. *Drat!* she thought with horror. *I don't remember putting the cat in the laundry with his kitty litter tray.* The carpet in her flat was pale cream which would change if the cat decided to contribute to its colour. Now panicky thoughts rampaged through her head as she imagined the worst. *He won't be able to get to his kitty litter.* She could hold that stress-fuelled fear all night unless *hmm…*she thought. *It will give me a good reason to go home early.*

She took a deep breath. *For heaven's sake she told herself, just forget the cat for the time being…*and then thought *It may well become* *a catastrophe!* She cringed to herself at this little pun. Lately she had been making more and more puns. 'Dad jokes', Jacquie called them. It wasn't a very clever pun anyway.

She would have to summon all of her fortitude to deal with the problem when she got home but for now it was too good a night to waste. She leant with one hand on the rail of the verandah and tilted her drink to her lips with the other, enjoying the champagne's pungent aromatic tang which warmed her soul.

She feasted on the sounds of raucous crickets, the loudness of which rivalled the laughing people and pounding music. At this moment, life wasn't so bad after all.

She became aware of someone at the end of the verandah and her curiosity was aroused. She was good at picking up body language, the kind most people didn't see. There was awkwardness about this person for he occasionally cleared his throat and changed his stance. Alice was too shy to say hello, and fearing that she would be directing her gaze in the completely wrong direction, chose not to look over and not even acknowledge them.

The person, a male person strode purposefully towards her, about to go inside the front door so she imagined.

'Lovely evening' said a slightly formal voice with a hint of shyness as he stopped right in front of her.

'Oh yes', smiled Alice politely but keeping her eyes lowered. 'It is really nice. These crickets are so loud and I wonder how such small creatures can make so much noise by rubbing their legs together.'

Alice went on. 'It just seems a bit far-fetched, but there you are it's a scientific fact. They compete well with the humans sound-wise...and maybe intellectually as well.' *No Alice,* she told herself. *Don't gabble about inanities otherwise he'll question your sanity. Try being an adult!*

I'm such an idiot! She winced inwardly.

'Is that a scientific fact – about them being smart?' asked the stranger.

'No...it's just my gut instinct,' she answered.

'They do have large heads, about the size of their abdomens' the mystery man acknowledged.

'Yes, there is a lot that can't be explained.' he said. 'I recently saw a nature documentary of a crocodile attacking an antelope. Suddenly a mother hippo came crashing out of the undergrowth and trampled the croc, then tried nudging and licking the antelope back to life. That's not survival of the fittest. It's not Darwinianism. She was helping or trying to help a completely different species from her own.'

'It must have been like that a long time ago.' contributed Alice. 'Maybe they all lived happily together without constantly murdering each other...'

The stranger was indeed strange, thought Alice, but refreshingly so.

He found her point of view struck a chord in his own belief system. She talked about the anomalies in widely accepted scientific theories.

Now she was on a roll and just couldn't stop talking. How bizarre – meeting someone who was a left fielder.

'Speaking of unexplained altruism in animals,' she said enthusiastically, 'I heard of a goldfish that had been damaged when it was young and it could only swim on the bottom and wasn't able to get to the top for the food. Another goldfish got under it and lifted it to the surface so that it could feed.'

'Truly amazing!' acknowledged the still unnamed man or boy or boy man. He continued: 'I was reading a National Geographic which had photos of a chained-up Husky dog and a Polar bear. Normally it's a pretty grizzly result. He gave a little laugh at his pun.

Alice took note thinking *'He may be a nerd.'*

He continued: 'The bear would have killed the dog instantly but there they were romping around and hugging each other as if they had known each other for years.

'Memories of Eden' murmured Alice mesmerised by the thought.

'Eden, oh yeah it was all perfect then.' said the male voice.

'By the way I'm Geoff.' he said.

'Oh, nice to meet you. I'm Alice.' said Alice politely. He grasped her hand and shook it, a strangely formal gesture she thought in today's casual society. *'I have probably said way too much!'* she grimaced inwardly. *And oh, I can't make my eyes meet his, and he'll know I'm blind. I just don't want to talk about it, especially with a complete stranger.*

She politely shook his hand, careful to keep her gaze down, and then returned to gazing over the verandah towards the garden.

Geoff looked at this gorgeous young woman, taking in her short ash-blonde hair, and her large blue eyes which would not meet his but gaze out always wander out toward the garden. She wouldn't meet his gaze, so he coughed uncomfortably, and pretended to look out towards the garden too. He wondered why she had been standing out here, alone. He also wondered if she had a husband or partner waiting for her back inside the loud chattering party.

'So how do you know Jacquie?' he asked.

Alice had a panicked moment where her heart dropped. 'We… we've worked together.' was all she said, simply. It was true, she told herself. He didn't have to know exactly in what capacity. 'And you?' changing the subject. Anything to avoid her blindness. For just one night she wanted to feel 'normal'. Her stomach churned. She hated to deceive anyone, but couldn't face 'that' conversation right now.

'How do you know Jacquie?' she asked.

'Went to Uni together.' he said. 'We studied a couple of Commerce subjects and were in the same tutes. Would hang out sometimes at the Uni Rec Bar, my mates were going out with some of her girlfriends. Same group you know?' he took a sip of his beer. 'We just kept in touch since then. She's a really good friend. I was so devastated went she had her accident…did you know her then?'

'No.' replied Alice, desperately wanting to change the subject. 'I've only known her since she's been in a wheel chair. ... she's one of my best friends.' *My only friend*, Alice thought. She had lost touch with most of her friends now.

'I just had to come out and enjoy this. I love getting close to nature.' she chattered, keen to change the subject. 'I know it's not the Blue Mountains, but it's all I can have at the moment.'

She took a leisurely sip from her drink.

'You should get out more if you think that this is living close to nature.' He said this in a way which she interpreted as being confrontational. She thought it out of keeping with what she knew so far of his gentle manner, but supposed that men can be thoughtless when they are (or they think they are) only being down to earth.

With a tinge of gentle sarcasm he said, 'So, are you a power-dressing executive during the day?' Alice could only wonder why he would say that, as she felt very far from being highly groomed.

He's obviously teasing me about my scruffy appearance.

'No.' she said, a tinge of annoyance in her tone.

Geoff continued, 'The only air you get comes through an air conditioner, so this suburban air smells great to you – even though it is mixed with a fair percentage of petrol fumes.' He paused. The crickets sang loudly to the stars that Alice couldn't see, though she gazed out towards them.

'I get clean air every day. I come from up near the Bogong

high plains.'

'Oh really?!' she said intensely and with genuine longing. Suddenly more interested in this person, she swept her gaze in the direction of his face. 'I would love to go to the mountains. I used to go,' she said, her voice trailing off as melancholy precious memories of her times with Stephen came clearly to her mind. They had trekked many a mile through dank eucalypt forest, so quiet and wild.

'Why don't you go?' asked Geoff. 'It's not far really.'

'I haven't wanted to go for a long time. The bush is so sad and well, it's lonely and I just don't feel the need to go any more.'

'Now that's the city slicker in you talking. You've got to get back to your roots, closer than a front verandah in the suburbs,' he said.

Alice felt trapped. She didn't want his sympathy but couldn't tell him why going to the bush was difficult for her. What could she say? *I could say shut up and leave me alone but I don't want to be left alone. I like talking to him. He's interesting but he is pushing me and I feel like I'm going over a waterfall soon!*

'Well, it's alright for you,' she burst out. 'I guess you can up and go anywhere, anytime you darn well like.' She felt heat flush her face.

He retaliated, in a half-joking way, 'I'm afraid you are a typical yuppie, always too busy to get away from their mobile phone reception, and to actually live!' With that he took a fast swig of his drink. He turned to walk away back to the party, but at that moment her heart wrenching sob pulled him suddenly back.

It was a shock to have someone she was enjoying talking to turn on her. *Damn these water works!* She wiped tears off her face and did the best she could to hide the fact that she was crying. Geoff looked down at her in even greater shock to see the pain he had caused her. He put his hand on her arm, and stared intently into her face. *This is really awkward,* he thought. She flinched and turned her head away. It suddenly dawned on him – and he could have kicked himself for not noticing before – that she was blind. He could now understand her charade and excuses. Deeply grieved he managed to stutter the words:

'You're blind, aren't you?"

'What do you think!' she snapped.

Her tears just wouldn't stop and it really annoyed her. She wished she was a bit more resilient. It embarrassed her to be so darn vulnerable. He offered her a hanky which (Alice thought with a strange surge of tenderness) was neatly ironed. Then she thought (with horror) that he may be a serial mother's boy which should not matter to her anyway as she was completely ambivalent towards him. Well completely ambivalent until what happened next.

He felt terrible, and rude. Normally he would never point out someone's disability in mid-conversation. He could have kicked himself (again).

'I am so sorry. Please don't cry,' he said softly. He hesitated for a moment, while Alice cried silent painful sobs into his hanky.

He awkwardly put his arm around her shoulder, and as her head drew close to his chest it did not disturb her as much as she would have expected.

Geoff cleared his throat, and said 'Most people put up with anything I say because they know I'm only joking. How could I be such a total yobbo?' and shook his head sorrowfully.

You are a man she thought in answer to his comment, and tried to pull herself together.

Men are notorious for it.

Why should I find this stranger so comforting? It's been ages since I cried in front of someone.

Suddenly she shuddered and recoiled. How could she ever be in another man's arms? *What's wrong with me! Plenty! But I don't even know him! I must be crazy – having a breakdown.*

Tears rolled down her face and sobs shook her whole body. After a few minutes, she pulled away, embarrassed, and sniffed hastily into the hanky. She was sure she was as red as a beetroot from crying, and she even wished she could give the hanky back, but obviously she couldn't! Hatred surged through her, and it was all for herself. How could she forget Stephen her dead fiancée even for a moment?

She felt faint, at the horror of almost filing away Stephen's precious memory in the back of the filing cabinet, maybe even right down the back never to be seen again! Falling into the arms of another man was tantamount to falling into bed with him in her rather puritanical eyes.

Meanwhile inside, the party went on. A wave of loud ribald laughter rent the air and Alice felt ill. She felt like a hooker because she had found the stranger comforting, feeling some of the tenderness she used to feel. She felt like she was betraying Steven the one whom she was going to marry. She was finding an outlet for her eight years of grief that had starved her of real closeness with anyone. She stoically punished herself feeling responsible for the whole abseiling disaster.

Give it a rest Alice! She admonished herself.

She knew on an objective level that she was innocent of any wrong doing but still remembered that day when she sat in the sun with a soft drink and a cream doughnut congratulating herself on not doing the crazy abseiling thing. She had even been reading a Woman's Day at the time, about the hardships of those celebrities glad that she had such a happy 'together' life. She hadn't been able to cosset and pamper herself again since then.

I could have stopped him from that stupid thrill-seeking stunt. He would have stopped for me. Geoff was unaware of her inner turmoil. He didn't know her painful history. Strong gentle hands placed on each of her arms, and Geoff said, 'I'm sorry for upsetting you, Alice. I've been a rude aggressive pig. I wish there was something I could do to make it up to you. I could kick myself for the stupid comment about yuppies which I don't think you are – and by the way if you are, I don't care. All I know is that you are the most interesting person I've met in years.' Alice sniffed, unable to think of anything to say.

'Would you like a cup of tea? How do you have it? It'll make you feel better.'

She almost said: 'Weak and white like my men.' but didn't know him well enough for that.

'White with no sugar, thanks very much' she answered, still feeling a bit silly over the crying.

She thought with a cruel dagger twisting through her heart. Why couldn't *he* be Stephen?

They sat on the porch. The crickets redoubled their musical efforts and were in full song. A curious elation welled up in her somewhere and she didn't know why. Maybe it was because she was feeling something real, something strong. Maybe it was because she felt for a moment again what it was like to be loved and adored. It was such a warm and magical feeling the feeling of being safe, cherished. Maybe she was being really dumb denying that she was feeling something for this hayseed boy.

After all he had already proved he could be insensitive. But he was interesting, he had a nice voice too. She didn't want him to feel he was so obnoxious that he caused her to cry with a simple jibe about being a city dweller.

Geoff brought the tea back out to the verandah. As they sipped their tea Geoff tried to make small talk. They chatted about their commutes – Geoff had driven a few hours to be here tonight. Alice had cabbed it only about half an hour. Geoff was nattering about the choices of restaurants in the city. He talked about the state of the roads and Melbourne town planning. On he went. *He's not a bad talker thought Alice, once he gets going. In fact, he is quite the chatty one* she smirked. She suddenly thought that she had better be polite and tune into what he was saying.

'So, since Uni, I became (don't hold it against me), an accountant. And I worked for the last eight or so years for firms in the city. I pretty much hated every minute of it. Forced to be with people day after day, who in real life you wouldn't dream of befriending. Many of them were the nasty, competitive types, vying for the boss's attention to become partners, and the pathetic office glory. I hated it. I missed the farm.' 'I hate that.' She said, and listened intently. She wished she could see him, what he looked like. His voice was rich, with a rich Aussie accent only found in the country. He sounded quite mature but with a youthfulness to his voice and manner. *How old must he be?* She imagined he had brown hair. *Oh, what am I doing?* She admonished herself, as Geoff continued.

'So last year, dad had a bit of heart trouble and so quit my job to help him. I moved back out to the country, and help dad run the farm…and in my spare time I train the horses.'

'Is your dad OK now?' Alice asked politely.

'Yep, he's fine – on a blood thinner and what not. Should be cutting down on the food side of things, but Mum isn't exactly helping him from that perspective. She likes to cook, put it that way…'

'What kind of farm do you have?' she asked sipping her tea, eager to get off the subject of his mother, and placing the cup on the saucer.

Geoff explained 'I'm sorry about the cup and saucer. It's a bit harder to use than a mug but Jacquie said we weren't allowed to use the mugs because she just got three sets of matching dinner sets and had to try them out on people.'

Gosh, a man interested in chinaware, I should photograph him, take him to the taxidermist and place him in the museum as an example of a rare species. She started giggling but thought it would be a bit cruel to tell Geoff this, and plus he would probably think she was weird (or weirder).

Geoff looked at her questioningly.

'It's nothing, nothing, said Alice waving her amusement away. 'Keep talking, I'm interested.'

'Now, yes back to your question. The farm. Well, we raise Hereford cattle, you know the red and white ones – you've probably seen them at...Oh, heck I'm sorry!' *'Don't* be sorry and don't feel you have to apologise for everything you say that has to do with seeing or having to see. I'm just not offended and I'd rather you expressed yourself without censoring your every comment for me!'

'Beef cattle', she said slowly 'so they aren't the ones that give milk?' she asked innocently.

Geoff gave a little chuckle 'No they are for meat but they obviously give milk to their calves.'

'Obviously!' said Alice trying to cover her ignorance. She did understand that calves would have to have milk but hadn't thought of it straight away. 'You have to explain everything to me in very simple terms because I *am* a yuppie after all!'

'Point taken,' smiled Geoff, 'I'll have to remember that but for a city slicker you are more interesting than most and by the way I am horribly ashamed of upsetting you and if there was some way of making it up to you I will.'

'Yeh, O.K, I'll make you pay.' said Alice slowly and also slowly twirling her hair and feeling uncomfortable, then suddenly she exclaimed: 'How cruel!' Mind you I *do* like a good T. bone steak. I guess that's how the meat starts out, by being *Alive!*'

'Yes, yes, that's true', Geoff laughed. He gazed at her smiling, rapidly finding her quite quirky and irresistible. 'I train the horses for endurance riding. I've been in the Quilty – the hundred-mile race – a few times but haven't won it yet. There is a sixty-miler coming up in a few weeks and I would really love to win it. Riding through the forest is great. It's so still and then a whip bird, or a bellbird will call. It feels like I'm in another world that has never changed since time began. It smells so clean, like eucalyptus. I feel like it could get all of the poisons from the city out of my system, sort of a degreaser. Alice was listening rapturously and asked him all sorts of questions about the horses and thought him to be really accomplished and very industrious to train horses as well as helping to run a farm. He really did have a good sense of humour but didn't seem too cynical about things, just healthily sceptical in the true Australian Way.

She placed both her hands around the cup and tried to soak all of its warmth into her. Even though it was late summer, with the coming of evening Melbourne was getting cold.

Geoff noticed. 'Are you cold?' I've got a jumper you can borrow, but it's probably got horse hair all the way through it and it probably stinks a bit horsey too,' he said with a laugh.

'My favourite fragrance – Equus!' she smiled at his thoughtfulness. She liked his manners and consideration. It was gentlemanly.

'Don't worry I'm alright for the moment. I can cope with much worse Melbourne weather. It's so true what they say about Melbourne weather – four seasons in one day. I started off in a T-shirt but now we've had a quick change of season, back to winter.' She hugged her arms despite playing the tough girl.

'You've got goose bumps. Let me get the jumper, please!' He sounded almost distressed to see her shivering.

'Oh, very well, if you insist,' she said regally with teeth chattering.

'Yes, I *do* insist and don't think you're fooling anyone. Your lips are turning blue!' he answered.

She heard him crunch across the gravelly driveway, and then he was back.

'Here you go. You'll have to roll the sleeves up a bit, otherwise they'll get in your tea.' He carefully rolled up the sleeves and adjusted her collar in a motherly tender way, normally something that Alice would find annoying, being so independent and proud. But Alice felt her heart flutter as if it was melting in warm butter.

She suddenly wanted to run away, but part of her also wanted to stay. She didn't want to tell him why she had to get home before ten on a Saturday night. That may make him feel a bit sick – the story about the catastrophe on the carpet – and it would certainly show off her helplessness. Heck he would probably come home and clean up the cat poo if she asked him but she just couldn't bear that.

'Excuse me Geoff. I'll be back in a minute.' she said and then went inside and rang a taxi. She came back out to the verandah and then sat for a while chatting comfortably with Geoff until she heard it pull up in the driveway.

Geoff stood up when she stood up much alarmed. 'I would have driven you home you know,' he said with disappointment.

'It's OK. I like to do things for myself and you don't even know me and…It wouldn't be fair to drag you away from all this *fun*! You can enjoy the overachiever's club.' she said flippantly. 'Look, forget that. You know I don't mean that! I'm only joking. I'm not *that* mean!'

'I'm getting used to you,' said Geoff warmly. 'And I think you *are* probably *that* mean.' 'You stick the little barb in. It's quite normal. Most people I know and especially the ones on the land are like that.' said Geoff.

She sniffed imperiously. 'Landed gentry or bushwhackers? I like to think that the barbs I stick in my victims don't discriminate. I've spent my night avoiding people so I haven't been caustic to anyone tonight except maybe to you – landed gent of landed gentry fame! I'm a fine one to talk. At least now you can mingle with others.'

'It's normal to be more comfortable with some people and not others.' said Geoff comfortingly. Thinking to himself that he was privileged she felt comfortable talking to him virtually all evening. 'I'm like that, everyone's like that. You can't be your true self with everyone. We have to put on special manners for some people and can be downright disgusting with others. That's life Alice. I don't judge you.'

'Anyway, I'm not interested in meeting anyone else. It wouldn't matter if I left now. I've met you and that's all that matters.' he said.

Alice felt a little flush of joy at his flattery but felt a feeling that she had heard these exact words on some romantic film – something with Colin Firth in it.

'I hope I haven't scared you off with my rural ramblings,' he said sadly.

'You can talk all night about the country and I'm all ears. Really! I had a lovely time and, oh!' she smiled and turned quickly to face him.

'Here, can you help pull this jumper off for me. I know it's a nice one and probably knitted by a loving mum who would be mortified if you loaned it to a complete stranger.' She placed her bag down, and peeled the bulky garment over her head.

'Are you sure you won't need it?' he asked.

'Don't worry. I'll be warm in the taxi. In the old days I would probably have been engulfed in cigarette smoke' she answered.

Alice got up to leave and Geoff went to touch her hand. She felt his warmth brush past her, but pulled away.

'Bye,' she said and started tapping her way across the front lawn.

'Hey!' he called. 'Your bag, you've left it here!'

'Oh!' laughed Alice, 'My bag must have been surgically removed because bags and I are inseparable.' She gave a little laugh and thought how nice it was to really laugh for a change.

'Women and their handbags, mystery of the ages' said Geoff sagely.

'Don't knock it!' exclaimed Alice. 'Men put as much junk in their wives and girlfriend's bags as the women do. Think about it. There are keys, wallets and mobile. I'm making a point here!'

'Capiche!' ('I understand!' in Russian) said Geoff feeling very clever.

'Capiche as well.' giggled Alice.

'See you,' answered Geoff wistfully, and quietly waved. He watched as the headlights faded from the driveway and flooded the quiet suburban street. With a roar it was gone. Inside him a light had gone out. She had pulled away from him when he went to touch her hand. Maybe she found him repulsive. *I probably stunk like the horses he thought cringing. Mind you to me that's a good smell. Maybe I was on the manure side of horse smell. She had worn it but was probably too polite to complain on the smell of the jumper. I wore it all day.* He gave a curious sniff to the under arms of his jumper which, he had now put on and headed inside.

Jacquie pulled him aside in the entrance hall.

'So, you met my little Alice?' said Jacquie. 'Quite a lovely girl and but somewhat of a whinger.'

Geoff laughed and shook his head. 'Who isn't? She's funny… feisty. She's great!'

'So why so down in the mouth Godfrey?' asked Jacquie, using her nickname for him.

'Just ignoramus farmboyitis,' he said 'and a horse manure aftershave.'

Three

Days passed, interminably so and Alice found, whilst working on her assigned tasks at the Rehabilitation Centre, her thoughts drifted occasionally to that nice country boy/gentleman who was really not so quiet once he got going. He could talk as much as the average drunken Joe but without the accompanying maudlin slurring comments such as:

'What's the matter love? You know what you have to do? You have to loosen up, have fun' Alice resented losers who relied on alcohol to have the courage to tell her how to be happy when they were chronically unable to manage their own lives.

'Christianity is a crutch,' they would say to her. Alice would seethe barely able to control herself from saying: 'Certainly, and what's your crutch then, a belly full of alcohol?' But she wouldn't say it. No! because that would be rude and it could hurt some ones feeling. Suddenly she didn't want to be 'nice'. Given a cricket bat she would gladly whack someone with it. Now that definitely wouldn't be nice but it sure would 'hit' the spot (she chuckled at her clever coincidence).

To be drunk is often the only way an Aussie guy can relax enough to talk or open up and or meet a girl. Opening up to a drunken bloke has the danger value of opening up an oyster with a pocket knife.

If you don't gouge a hole in hand, you can still be in for a case of food poisoning. At face value they can both look OK. No, it's better to leave men's deeper feelings well enough alone – presuming they have some.

She smiled as she remembered the neatly ironed hanky Geoff had given her to snivel into after she *cried*! First time in public for years!

How could she! What a loser! And that jumper, oh she would never forget that. It was warm and soft apart from the odd, prickly horse hair here and there. She felt a sharp sweet stab in her heart as she remembered the tenderness of his embrace when she cried and the way he had groomed her, arranged her collar and sleeves like he was an old mother hen. The lovely aroma of jumper set her mind racing, as she imagined Geoff riding across craggy mountain ridges on one of his endurance horses. *What a wonderful sport. He thought that his jumper offended me but I breathed it in like incense, essence of equus.*

I just love horses!

'How are you going, you old bag?' said Jacquie cheerfully as she rolled up. Alice smiled and set down the glue that she was using to assemble a peg basket.

'I'm just fine Jacquie, but I'll be glad to get back to the Braille writer. This glue is withering up my hands. Every time I peal the glue off them, I'm making a complete cast of my hand like you do with those face masks.'

'Which were taken off the market because they cause facial hair growth.' interjected Jacquie.

'On a similar note,' said Jacquie, 'I have a friend…'

'Good for you.' interrupted Alice.

'…a friend who is nicer than you by far, by the way…and… *who* was very pregnant (do you have to interrupt?' said Jacquie continuing, 'My friend was in the bath and asked her mum to wash her back because she couldn't reach it. Her mum, always the willing slave started to wash it with soap. 'Use a cleanser.' said my friend because I have a pimply back.'

'Do I know this person?' asked Alice.

'It's classified! Will you just *listen*!" snapped Jacquie. 'Anyway,' she continued: 'The mother of my pregnant friend in the bath, said 'Oh, OK well do you want me to use the face milk on your back?'

Then my pregnant friend in the bath said: 'No that would be back masking'.

Jacquie waited for the laugh.

Alice didn't react, not even a smile. 'Is that true? It's pretty funny but is it true?'

'*You* know', said Jacquie 'When they play records backwards and get a satanic message.

That's called back masking.'

There was silence for a few seconds and Alice could only shake her head and smirk at Jacquie's story. It was so bizarre that it had to be true but with Jacquie it was hard to tell because sometimes she really spun whoppers.

'Who do you think my class would actually want to make these lousy things, these peg baskets? These hands are as dry as parchment. If I rubbed them together long enough the friction might start a fire.'

Jacquie smiled, amused. 'Well, I suppose the therapy is in the making of them, not in the peg baskets themselves…Or maybe the therapy is in peeling the glue off your hands.' 'You're the only one I can complain to Jacquie. The others think I'm quiet and long suffering but I want you to know the real me. You should be flattered that I would be so up front with you. Frankly this gluing is getting to me and it's all over the floor, isn't it?

Isn't it? I know!'

'Yes, Alice there is a little bit on the floor but have a good cry and you'll feel better. Will you just get a grip of yourself and shut up for two seconds? For a private person you really spill your guts to me. Lucky me! So anyway – what did you think of my party? Hey did your cat get to his litter the night of the party or did you *cat*apult him out of the window?'

'Oh, I'll never live down the cruelty to the cat incident, will I? Not with you around. You just don't know how aggravating he can be. He meows and meows for food every waking minute except when he sleeps on things and leaves shards of fur all over my flat!'

'Did he get to the kitty litter?' asked Jacquie.

'Yes, he did but he scratched the door to pieces to do it. Why I keep a cat I'll never know.

Heck I can barely look after myself!'

'You,' stated Jacquie, are the craziest I've ever seen you, and I think I like it...*and* I think I know what's making you so touchy Alice. Anything's better than being depressed.

This rage is what is keeping you going, so if it works, I would say keep it up.' Alice complained, 'I'll have to get some Polyfilla or paint to fix it up. Actually, the landlord is coming to inspect the flat this week and I haven't done anything about the door. He was good enough to let me keep the cat – probably sorry for me because I'm blind – and I don't think he with will be overjoyed to see the door shredded like a ribbon-gum.'

Jacquie looked up slyly planning something. She was glad that Alice couldn't see her face full of machination and had to be careful because her voice might give her away. As casually as she could she commented: 'Look, I'll send Geoff over. Remember Geoff at the party – you two met? I'll send him around. He's handy, and he's in town this week doing business for his dad – a cattle sale, I think. I've got all the stuff, you know, the poly filler and paint-white paint. They're all white doors in your place so hopefully it will be the same shade of white. Geoff is a bit of a Boy Scout and loves to help damsels in distress so don't be nasty to him, not that I'm asking you to be too nice either. I wouldn't expect it of you. He'll be happy with a cup of tea and a biscuit. And no don't you dare cook any!'

'But, but...' stammered Alice, trying to get a word in. 'I don't know him well enough to ask him to do this for me. He'll think I'm needy and pathetic and it's not fair that you make these arrangements without consulting me, and why shouldn't I make biscuits?' 'Things are really bad aren't they. He won't think you're needy and pathetic unless you start whining. As for making these arrangements without consulting you, I'm consulting you now! Do you want the door fixed or not? He can do it and he'll probably like being useful, being a hero. Boys from the bush when they're back in town are always good to make use of. Will Sunday at eleven be O.K?' Jacquie sucked in a breath after her long monologue.

'I...er don't know.' stammered Alice.

Not waiting for an answer Jacquie took off and yelled cheerily 'Anyway I've gotta go now – see ya.' She nimbly swung her chair around and wheeled away at high speed, knowing that Alice was sure to think of a dozen reasons why Geoff, the so-called 'stranger' (who she had talked to for most of the party) couldn't come into her home. Jacquie had to make a quick getaway. She giggled, and whispered to herself 'yessss' and gave a little triumphant punch in the air.

Bewildered, Alice could only say 'But...'

Her jaw hung open and she quickly wiped the glue off her hands. It had overflowed and gone onto the floor as she had listened powerlessly to her fast-talking friend. She shook her head and grimaced as she fixed up the tacky mess on the floor. 'What a little meddler. Look at the mess she's got me into!' she muttered through gritted teeth. 'She just ran over me with her strong personality.' Alice smirked and frowned at the same time.

That night she exfoliated opaque glue sheets in an almost a perfect cast of her hand.

New kitchen gloves! She smiled with hideous intrigued.

The morning that Geoff was to come, Alice went crazy and scurried and hurried and flurried *and* cooked biscuits, the very thing Jacquie told her not to do. Her little abode was indeed humble. Her parents lived in Townsville and had only been able to visit once in the last two years. Running a banana farm wasn't conducive to having holidays. They were bananas, and didn't need milking twice a day like a cow but there was plenty to do to produce a ripe healthy crop.

They wanted her to come with them to live in Townsville, but pride and a wish to punish herself had kept her in this rather sad social backwater. Also, she didn't think she could go back to a small town. Here in Melbourne at least she had the facility of the Rehabilitation Centre where she could work, and plenty of distractions like the trains which rattled by at regular intervals. Many said of course that the rail system wasn't streamlined enough, but Alice would beg to differ and could practically feel it in her bones when the next train was going to rattle by. *That's the price I had to pay to be close to the Rehabilitation Centre.*

Dad had repainted the flat a nice bright white, (so I'm told) but the smoky atmosphere of the city has dulled it to a yellowy cream, (so I haven't been told but have guessed) No-one would ever tell me that unless they were completely tactless. Hang on, actually I think Jacquie did.

Alice felt annoyed as she plumped cushions on her old couch, and vacuumed the carpet. How would she know if the place was tidy or not? It wasn't very satisfying not being able to admire the fruits of her labour. Now she sat. The clock ticked by second by second at ten then a bit later a quarter to eleven. Would he be late? She hoped he would be late, hoped he wouldn't come at all and then she hoped that he would. After all she had gone to a lot of trouble for him. He'd better come! How dare he not! Alice snorted and pushed her fringe of out of her face. *The last time I made biscuits? The same time Haley's Comet was in town. Or was it a blue moon? Whenever I made them isn't the point. It's the thought that counts and the effort! I hope he appreciates that!*

What if a pair of her undies was lying on the floor or a chunk of toothpaste spit in the bathroom sink? Despite her most meticulous efforts, such things could be there that she preferred not to be seen may be seen. She knew he would pretend not to notice anything vile and she knew he wouldn't tell her if he had. Heck if he did tell her that would be worse. She just hoped that there wasn't anything to notice but she knew a stray hair could spoil everything or maybe she was being childish and prudish about this. If he liked her surely Geoff would overlook these things. It had been a long time since she actually cared what someone thought of her appearance or housekeeping. *And anyway,* she thought, *so what if he doesn't like me. I couldn't care less.*

But she did care, and that is what unnerved her so.

Coming from the country she was sure he'd seen worse. He'd told her about the copious mucous coming from a cow's nose and the unbelievably long pink tongue delving right up the nostril to drag out and eat it. That was one of the intriguing things he had to say at Jacquie's party. It made her old toothpaste spit seem like chicken feed – and maybe chooks would eat it. *Stop this ridiculous thinking!* She felt nervous and almost wished that he wouldn't turn up at all. Almost…but he was quite nice…to talk with.

The inevitable knock came, and Alice felt herself stiffen and her stomach dropped several metres below the ground. She walked to the door, took a deep breath and slowly turned the knob. Her heart pattered away making her feel the flight or fight response. She was nothing but an alarmed impala and she felt like she might just leap out of a window, run clear out of Melbourne and head for the Darling Downs – a fitting savannah like home for a nervous creature like herself where she could hide in long grass.

'Hello,' she said with face lowered slightly trying to sound a little nonchalant. *This is ridiculous I don't have to behave like I'm a nervous debutante seated against the wall waiting for her first invitation to dance! Heck I hardly know the guy but darn he makes me feel so good and yet I'm terrified of letting him down.*

'It's me, Geoff, from Jacquie's party. Remember? You wouldn't forget me in a hurry because I'm the only bloke you know who carries an ironed handkerchief. I'm here to fix you're your door… do you mind holding the door open, I've got a whole load of fix-it stuff here?'

Please! Hold the door please? How civil! Yes of course, it's the least I can do! she thought 'Will the neighbours go crazy about the sander? I brought an extension cord too. You do get cranky old fossils from time to time wanting their peace and quiet despite the fact that they may have an annoyingly loud budgie or listen to the races with the radio turned up full bore.'

'Great…about the extension cord and if the neighbours complain about the noise, you can set the blue heeler onto them.' she laughed.'

'You know, not all farmers own a blue heeler following at heel all the time!' he laughed. Alice smiled and nodded with a flick of her hair, trying to give the impression of nonchalance. 'My neighbours make a racket every day of the week so I don't think they have the right to go mental over a sander.'

'Well,' sighed Geoff it shouldn't take long and it's not like it's seven in the morning.' Geoff surveyed the damage to the door. 'That's nothing!' I'll fix this *cat*egory three cat damage and your landlord will be none the wiser.'

'That's a pretty good 'cat' joke…for a country bumpkin.'

Geoff held his hands up pretending to protect himself. 'You're a pretty fierce creature today, aren't you?' he laughed delighted to get a reaction from her. 'Don't be too fierce or I'll run away.'

Alice had to stop herself from saying 'Your jokes are a *cat*alyst for my vitriol' but she wasn't sure that it might think her condescending and pompous Why make an issue out of everything. He would think for sure that she was keen on him if she bantered with too much abandon and gaiety. She didn't have the energy. Why did she have to behave in any way for anyone anyway? She couldn't quite get her head around that but she enjoyed teasing him and he probably did too because whatever she said seemed to bounce off him and cause him to make a kind of snickering chuckle noise.

Alice sat on the couch and listened to the tapping, the sanding and then the squelching noises as Geoff mixed the filler and then the paint. There was the waiting period. The filler had to dry, so they sat around for quite a while. The silence was ringing in her ears and she felt nervous and was mortified when her innards created a sound very like a brown bear.

'There's a bear in there.' laughed Geoff, copying the words of the Playschool theme song.

'But I don't think there's a chair as well.' sniggered Alice, again copying the next line of the song and feeling grateful that Geoff wasn't horrified by her loud bodily noise. Geoff must have heard worse on the farm, and didn't care at all saying: 'Oh is that you? I thought it was me.'

After a while the filler dried. Thank *God! I can't control all of this gas! I could run my whole house's power needs with it.*

'I really appreciate this Geoff,' she said as she heard the slap and smooth of the paint going on. 'I couldn't have done it myself.'

'Of course not, and why should you when you have a willing slave at your disposal. I don't mind doing things like this… especially for you.' He added quietly. *'What* did you say?' she asked (knowing full well what he had said) 'Especially for you?'

'Especially for you, for you, special price' answered Geoff cheekily in a badly performed Italian accent.

Alice laughed and colour rushed to her face. She loved his sweet little sayings but didn't really know how to cope with them other than to joke back, as she had never had terms of endearment directed towards her even from her fiancé. 'Gosh,' she said placing her hands on her cheeks, 'I'm hot!'

'You certainly are!' he said with just the faintest hint of innuendo.

Alice smiled knowing exactly what he meant. A saucy little compliment.

'I'll let you know when it's payback time.' he said and he kept painting. 'For fixing this door, I mean. A block of fruit and nut chocolate would be good.'

'Fruit and nut chocolate, I'll remember that' said Alice suddenly being earnest.

'Only kidding!' said Geoff 'I don't like chocolate at all actually. You can pay me in some other way, don't worry I'll keep thinking about it.'

Geoff was too busy to notice her blushing but he wasn't too busy to keep up a volley of cheeky remarks designed to make her smile. He wanted to make her happy but he was also sensitive enough to stop if it got out of hand or nasty. He hoped that someday his brotherly banter could be replaced by something more romantic.

But then again, a lot of his mates kept their interminable Aussie sarcasm well into married life much to the chagrin of their partners. He wanted more but didn't want to frighten her off. He was enjoying the interaction with her and liked the way she gave as good as she got. This was a sport they both enjoyed – teasing, tormenting, but only because they liked each other so much. It tended to fuel his attraction for her. It was best not to get too philosophical and just get on with this job. Maybe, he thought, it was the paint fumes winding him up, making him a stand-up comedian. If he was no good Alice would start throwing rotten fruit at him.

'If you get sick of me and my sense of humour you are welcome to throw rotten fruit at me.'

'I hope you are not assuming that because I'm blind I have rotten fruit at my disposal!' she exclaimed.

Quick, back pedal! Geoff gulped.

'It's just a saying. It's always rotten fruit.'

'Mmm. I think you're right. The next time you come here I'll make sure I keep some for you. Would rotten pumpkin do? I always have plenty of that.'

'Sure Alice, I'd be honoured.'

Both got a little snigger out of that one.

Alice did a bit of nervous housework and for the first time in her life was happy to be sweeping a floor. She had a strong aversion to people pitying her or helping her but she couldn't help him doing what he was doing. She went to the kitchen, placed a handful of biscuits on the plate and then took it into her lounge room. She had made a pot of tea and was a bit nervous shaking a little as she poured it.

'Here', said Geoff, 'Let me do that!'

'No really I can do it – it's fine.' she answered.

Geoff took a biscuit and bit into it with a 'Mmmm, delicious, really delicious!' 'Really, are they?' exclaimed Alice in delight. She tried to hide her grin which was trying to stretch from ear to ear.

'Yep, great' said Geoff, 'Nearly as good as my mums!' He was being cheeky. 'Nearly, really?' said Alice coolly missing the humour intended. She was already starting to think that Geoff may be mother's little apron wearer.

'I don't think you realise what a compliment that is!' he said enthusiastically.

Geoff saw her face drop. He had gone too far. He could say what he liked about her but not about her cooking. *Oh, I could kick myself he thought. What am I going to say now about that? Is there way out…or not?*

There was nothing to do but make excuses. 'You're wrong if you think I'm a mummy's boy. I only said that to stir you up. I wouldn't tease you unless I really liked you. You *are* the best cook this side of the black stump. And if you have to know I'm grateful for any food homemade or not. In fact, I think I've said too much. Your biscuits are perfect, a little spicier than mum's…

'That's the cinnamon.' said Alice perking up.

'Mum's are more bland.' he said really throwing his dramatic self forward. 'In fact, I think I've said too much.'

'You haven't said enough.' said Alice flouncing off towards the kitchen (It's hard to flounce effectively when you are blind but she did look a little haughty and hurt.)

'Oh Alice, darn it I'm sorry' gushed Geoff.

'What can I do to make it better?' he pleaded.

'Ha! I've got you!' Alice said swinging around with an impertinent victorious grin and a fork in her hand pointing in his direction. Geoff laughed despite himself.

'So, you wash, fold and iron your own cloths, help with the dishes and make your own bed?' Alice asked casually but with a slight smirk which Geoff noticed straight away. 'Yes and no' answered Geoff a little uncomfortably.

'Well,' he said sheepishly 'I do the wiping of the dishes quite a lot. I usually make my bed and no I don't wash and fold and iron my clothes, very often. I'm an only child and,' he said, and added plaintively 'and she won't let me do it!' Alice raised her eyebrows, cooling slightly. Geoff went on.

'I mean, I lived on my own ever since Uni days...that's a good 12 years...I've only been back at home with my parent's for about a year – since dad had troubles with his health.'

'You don't know how to work the washing machine, do you! said Alice jokingly, but with a touch of steel in her voice.

Geoff sighed and wiped his forehead with his neat hanky and changed the subject.

'I hate earl grey tea, don't you?' They sat in opposite chairs sipping tea, which was English Breakfast.

'It tastes like perfume' added Alice going on to ask:

'Don't you think Melbourne's the tea drinking capital of the world outside England?' Geoff opened his mouth to answer when she asked: 'Do you want another biscuit? I haven't cooked them for about eight years.'

He really hated to be asked another question when you are half way through answering the previous one.

'I hope they're not eight years old! On the farm mum makes biscuits every week, but I think she enjoys it.' He said quickly hoping that this excused his mum baking so regularly – the fact that she enjoyed doing it.

Alice raised her eyebrows in amazement 'I can't believe that anyone would want to cook for recreation.'

'I'm struggling to understand,' she looked pensive. 'To become a lover of biscuit baking, one would have to have no other interesting things to do.' I would rather walk or run or ride or sail or, well…just about anything else. You can lose track of what you really like to do if you have switched off for a long time. Do you know what I mean?' 'Sort of,' Geoff answered getting the feeling that this was the start of a deep and meaningful interaction with Alice but felt he may be going to sail off the end of the world. He didn't know her that well and it was wrong to assume she believed the world to be round. These were unchartered waters. He was happy to be in serious interaction and in regard to his mum and biscuits said: 'Mum just loves to cook and that's her passion. Heck some people get off on Trigonometry. It's all relative to what you enjoy doing and there is endless variety in that. I do what I like most of the time.'

'So, it seems' said Alice under her breath.

'If there's something I don't like doing I get it over and done with early otherwise I feel guilty. I wasn't much of a student at Uni but I got through it by hook and by crook, just kept plugging away at it.'

'As you know, I'm actually an accountant'

Alice smirked as he went on.

'I know, as I said before – don't hold it against me. But I'm happiest on the farm. It's a lot of work, but still, it feels like a permanent holiday and it's a good break from all of that office garbage – mind you there is some book-keeping, paperwork and what not to keep on top of. But it's different. I'm taking it day by day, as I don't know when or if Dad will be able to work the farm and train the horses on his own again. I'm loving it.'

He swigged his tea.

'Why didn't you do it from the start? I mean, what made you go to Uni to do accounting of all things? Didn't you want to do what your dad did?' she asked, interested in this man who seemed too nice – *too nice to be genuine. Surely, he had some baggage? Like me?* she thought.

'Dad actually encouraged me to go. He didn't think there was any sense in following in his footsteps during a drought. Mind you that was years ago and we've had a good amount of rain since then. I was excited about getting away to the city, getting independence. I don't regret it. But now, I'm just loving being back in the bush…I think my heart really is there.'

'It must be hard for you having a job you don't like. The things I don't like doing I do first to get them over and done with.'

'Oh, are you an obsessive compulsive?' Alice asked.

'No', answered Geoff 'Just a delayed gratification kind of guy.'

'I like a bit of discipline in my life, a bit of routine but I'm not going to wash my hands for half an hour after cleaning a stable for fear I'll catch horse worms!'

'Ooh creepy!' exclaimed Alice horrified.

'So,' asked Alice, 'Does delayed gratification mean that you are doing your boring job of fixing my door first putting the enjoyable cattle sale off till later?'

'Just the opposite! *You* are my gratification.'

'Pardon me! Alice retorted, laughing 'but that sounds a little...well?'

'You are much more interesting than a cattle sale if that's what you're wondering.'

'Alice, I don't have a clue what you're on about.' laughed Geoff.

'You seem to bring out the *bad* in me,' said Alice in delight.

'And I think you like that,' laughed Geoff.

'Of course, I do. It's just my laugh that puts me off laughing, it's such a hideous guffaw.' 'It is actually.' said Geoff with amusement shook his head then kept talking. 'Don't get me wrong. I love cattle sales, one of my favourite things about keeping stock – I get to combine my 'numbers' skills and background, with my love of the farm...But this time I was keen to get it over and done with because I knew my next stop was your place.'

'And you couldn't resist mucking around with a bit of spackle.'

'That's right, I'm always partial to a bit of spackle.' Geoff said quietly shaking his head at her cheekiness and responded in kind.

'It's called having a spak-attack.' she said.

He looked at her as though she was someone falling in mud on the funny video show. Alice was aware that suddenly all went quiet. She was starting to get the impression that she was an amusing treasure in his eyes and it made her a bit embarrassed. She sensed him paying intense attention to her. There seemed to be so much joy and goodness in him whereas she was bitter and miserable in actual fact. If he really knew her! She drifted away into negative gear, when she heard his voice again, reaching her. 'Yes, I do hate my job.' Alice went on. 'I mean, it's not what I grew up thinking I'd want to do as a little girl – yes I'd like to type up Braille documents and run therapy classes gluing peg baskets.'

This was a first hint to Geoff that Alice had not, in fact, been born blind.

'And there's the monotony of it all. I mean, nothing ever changes you know?...I just keep doing the same old thing day after day...But I guess I should look on the positive.' A train went past. The clock ticked. The cat began to yowl for food.

As the clattering of the train passed by, Geoff looked at the lovely young Alice. Her ash-brown hair, shiny and choppy...she was pale and looked as though she hadn't seen the sun in many years. She bit her lip, her clear blue eyes focused downwards. She was so young, but there seemed a lifetime of sadness that hung about her. Geoff sat on her worn frayed couch, looking at her from across her scratched coffee table, in her small flat with the faded white walls, and couldn't stand it anymore. He couldn't bear to leave her alone here. He found himself saying: 'Look, Alice – why don't you come with me this afternoon? Come to the mountains. God knows you need to get out of here. You have to get a bit of clean air into you, and listen for the sounds of the lorikeets and the plovers and the kookaburras. I could take you down to the trout stream and we could just sit and listen to the water. You'd love it. The grass smells so sweet there, and walnut trees smell really spicy. It's the sort of thing you just can't get in the city.' 'I could take you riding high along the mountain spurs through the valleys of manna gums up to the snow plain. What do you say Alice...Alice what do you reckon?' Alice was in her own little world becoming more morbid all the time. She, despite her bluff of arrogance still felt futile, inferior to Geoff who was the eternal optimist or so it seemed to her. *How could I ever make someone like Geoff happy when I'm so gloomy and self-absorbed. He loves the bush (and so do I) and he is so keen to tell me all about it in minuscule detail which I don't mind but how can I enjoy it with him when I am blind. If I had my sight, I would happily talk about it but I'm, too depressed to really listen. He doesn't know just how much of the bush I understand. I was part of that life once and full of it but now,* she hesitated and sadly thought *now it's all gone like Stephen.* Geoff's voice reached her again.

'Alice, are you listening to me? wakey, wakey!'

Alice did pay attention, snapped out of her introspection. and asked 'What, what's up Geoff? I told you I was and am rude and was thinking about something else. I didn't hear you properly. I know you love the mountains and streams and things. I did once too.'

'Alice.' said Geoff in exasperation: 'I asked you to come back with me now, today, to the farm, *please*? The bush is the place for you right now. It's so calm, and days go by much slower than they do here in the city without rushing, as if they'll never end. You say that you used to love it and you probably still do if you'd just *come away*! You could really let it all hang out. I would make sure you have a holiday, a real holiday where all you have to do is have fun and just relax. Goodness knows the sound of a busy city keeps you uptight. Fair dinkum once you've been on the farm a few days you'll forget what you had to have in the city. I think I know you Alice (although I haven't known you a long time) and I reckon when you get to feed a poddy calf you'll be totally won over.

'A poddy what?' Alice was intrigued.

'A calf, a poddy calf.' said Geoff enthusiastically. 'Sometimes the mother dies or for some reason can't feed the baby, and you have to feed it milk out of a bucket. Have you ever fed one?' asked Geoff.

'No', said Alice 'but I can imagine how cute it would be.'

'If you put your hand out it will suck the fingers on your hand. Their tongue is rough and feels like sandpaper or Velcro.'

'If you come to the bush with me, I promise this will melt your little hard heart!'

'Mmmm.' Alice said thinking about the dear little calf sucking her fingers. 'If you come with me, you will miss that train coming past every five minutes. How could you stand that!?' he laughed.

'Yes, the bush is a tantalising place and a smorgasbord of smells.' she said in a detached almost dreamy voice.

Geoff shook his head again at her quirky comment. He wondered if she was saying unusual words to stump him, show him up to be stupid, or whether that was the way she really liked to communicate. She was quite different.

Alice sat quietly, contemplating for a moment looking like she actually was going to say yes, then suddenly leapt up. Vehemently she said, 'No! I can't!' Now she went on, rattle, rattle, rattle, fast and slightly panic stricken. 'I can't go, because it's too short notice and I only just met you. What would people think of me, just running off with a complete stranger? Let's face it I've only just met you and you could be an axe murderer for all I know!'

Geoff smiled gently. 'Maybe I am,' he joked, in a menacing tone. 'Actually, I always carry a small hatchet in the back of the four-wheel drive You never know when you may feel the urge to hack someone to pieces. You know Alice, you've sized me up, you *know* my secret and as they say, now I'll have to kill you! Complete stranger, am I?' he said Geoff. 'Remember that you borrowed my jumper, one that my mum knitted. Not just anyone gets that privilege.' An amused glint came into his eyes and he smiled at tense little Alice whose hands were clenched together in her lap. She had suddenly run out of spunk. She seemed quiet and a little depressed. Perhaps it was too soon to ask her down to the farm but he had the most overwhelming desire to take her away from all this.

'And Jacquie can vouch for me.'

Alice looked pensive. She was thinking, hard.

'Lighten up lass, come on, give us a little smile.' he reached across the small coffee table and gently took her hand. 'This is something my Auntie would do when I was little.' He drew circles around her palm with his index finger saying: 'Round and round the garden like a teddy bear.' Then he walked in finger steps up her arm.

'One step, two step and tickly under there.' He then stopped at the top of her arm and gave her a little pat.

This all could have ended badly, thought Alice *Thank God he didn't go for the underarm even though it would have been perfectly safe. I put plenty of antiperspirant on this morning and I had shaved. I had a longish sleeved shirt on otherwise Geoff may have lost a hand to the vicious ferret than lives there.* She was finding it hard to remain serious. Obviously, Geoff was going out on a limb to comfort her but it all could have ended not actually in tears but in horrendous embarrassment.

Alice stiffened pursed her lips, set her jaw and tried to look serious, but before she knew it, she too was giggling like a two-year-old mainly at the thought about the ferret. This stunt of his was she thought exceptionally snaggish behaviour for a man, playing a childhood game with her but then again, he did seem different to most men she had met. Naturally she didn't tell him what she was just thinking but it came out anyway:

'You are truly insane.' And 'do you think I'm a two-year-old?'

'Well, you do seem to need plenty of pacifying and encouragement just like a needy little kid so I just thought this would make you smile. I'd give you one but then I think you would spit it.'

'What? Spit what?'

'A dummy.'

'How dare you!' Alice gave him a playful punch on the arm. Which caused him to grimace in genuine pain.

She didn't want to answer. She didn't want to say no, though. Changing the subject, Alice said 'So you're pretty close to your parents then?' Must be hard moving back in with them after all those years...does your mum know you've been loaning your jumper and hankies to complete strangers?'

'She's not a complete dragon you know – dad manages to live with her. I only try to keep her occupied with my washing and stuff, you know, to make her feel wanted.' 'You are so *thoughtful* Geoff!' said Alice arching her eyebrows. He was struck by her lovely face. Her lips formed a cute pink bow, and her cheeks looked soft.

Geoff rolled his eyes slightly, 'Yeah it's a challenge I admit. But it's not a long-term thing, as I said it was initially just to help Dad out. I've got my own house here in the city, and I've rented it out for now. But to be honest, I don't see myself living back her…I'm thinking I'll probably buy something closer to the farm or even build something nearby on the farm. Not quite sure yet.'

'Well, your mumsie would like that,' Alice said, unable to stop herself.

'Look, you seem to be obsessed with my mum and really she is just a usual adoring mum who…'

'Follows you around washing the hallowed mud from your work boots!' said Alice. 'As I was going to say' said Geoff (knowing he was going into the lion's den) 'she is an adoring mum who likes to cook and clean and wash and mend for her adorable son.' 'Enough!' shrieked Alice, 'I've heard enough! It could curl a suffragette's hair.'

'It's quite normal' said Geoff quietly with a glint in his eye, 'and you know while we are wasting all of this time talking, we or rather you could be packing to come with me to the farm and don't tell me that you're scared of my mum.'

'Sorry Geoff but she does sound dauntingly domesticated!'

'I'll take that as a positive because you wouldn't be saying anything nasty about my mother, would you?'

'No of course not but I am understandably nervous at the thought because she must really love you to do all of those things for you and she would be scrutinizing me to see if I am the kind of girl who would do the same picking up and cleaning and cooking for her son, a girl you are bringing home for her to *inspect.*'

'*Meet! meet!*' Said Geoff with mock disgust. 'She would be inspecting cattle not that she is that rapt in cattle but she would be *meeting* you.'

'Do you want to come or not Alice? I can only beg, cajole harass, urge.'

'Seriously Geoff' Alice said lowering her voice. 'Do you really think it's wise for me to go away with you? I've only met you twice. We haven't met for coffee or for anything else.'

Geoff groaned in protest.

'It's just that for you to ask me away to your farm is flattering and nice but I just don't know about it – is it right? I don't know.'

'You, Alice, are in need of a holiday and all I can say is that Jacquie can vouch for me. I really am a trustworthy type. I'll give you as much space as you need.'

'The guest room has a new ensuite.' Geoff said.

Alice's frown turned thoughtful.

'Hmm ensuite you say?' Alice rubbed her chin pensively. But really, she was thinking that the fact he was offering her a separate room was a good sign – that was what she was most concerned about. This set her mind more at ease.

'You're not quite convinced, are you? I can assure you that my parents are in the same house, and would hear any unusual goings on…although not that that would happen…I mean…you know what I mean,' he stammered.

'They might think it's just a possum on the roof,' said Alice, disarmed by his chivalry but not yet quite convinced.

'Hardly likely. That's a completely distinct sound and I should know because I had one living in the wall of my room when I was a kid.'

'Really?' said Alice amazed.

'Yeah, I used to feed it bread and it would take it in its little hand and eat it.' 'What did your room smell like?' asked Alice, a bit disgusted by the thought.

'Like possum,' said Geoff.

Fair enough, thought Alice.

'I think mum would like you because you appreciate my jumper. I almost had to leave home because I wrecked the first one she made me.'

'Do tell!?' exclaimed Alice keen to hear this juicy tidbit and half hoping to see a victory over indomitable Mrs Parker. She had never met the women but felt a little in awe of her because of the power she wielded in the family.

'You're a bit of a rebel, aren't you? You're looking forward to hearing about me and my mum clashing. I did something to that jumper she will perhaps never forgive. She almost didn't cook dinner for me and dad that night.'

'Oh, that must have been *some* transgression!' exclaimed Alice patronizingly. *Here she goes again with the big words* thought Geoff. *Couldn't she just say something simpler like stuff up.*

'I've done worse to my jumpers than loan them. I once washed one huge cable knit really carefully with dissolved soap flakes in lukewarm water. I rinsed it thoroughly and then…yeh well, (this is where the story gets freaky) I put it in the clothes-drier, on the *hot setting!'*

'After a while we could hear a distinct thumping noise and it was the jumper. When it came out it had shrunk and would have fitted a one-year-old baby but it was as heavy as a bag of cement. You're smiling. Is that allowed?'

Alice frowned with her brows, but her mouth curved up despite herself and she stifled a giggle.

'That was really great!' exclaimed Alice. 'It has really cheered me up, it's priceless! How could anyone do something so stupid?'

'Yeah,' chuckled Geoff as he remembered the incident, 'It thumped around in the dryer like a dead body.'

'There you go again talking about dead bodies. How can I go anywhere with a body snatcher? But what's more frightening is that you actually know what a cable knit jumper *is* let alone how to wash one!'

'Is that a hanging offence? Back to the interrogation…Well, *will* you?' he pleaded. 'I think you need a needier tone in your voice because I can't see your face.' said Alice as regal as Cleopatra.

Geoff ignored this last comment and continued: 'We could even get a doctor's certificate to say you need a well-earned rest. What fossil in the rehabilitation centre would demand you stay to make up the quota of peg baskets?'

'Nice of you to ridicule my job.' said Alice dark as a brewing storm with hints of thunder and electricity ready to strike out at any time.

Geoff didn't notice and said with a low laugh, 'I could arrange for you to have a little accident that may require a few days off work. You might need a doctor's certificate as long as you didn't spill the beans as to how it happened'

'And how would it happen Geoff?'

'I can give a fairly nasty Chinese burn.' he laughed.

'Violence won't be necessary,' said Alice slowly pursing her lips and staring upwards deep in thought. Geoff smiled broadly. She looked very solemn and folded her hands but to him she looked like a lost girl and all of his protective instincts went out to her. She did this for a minute that seemed to go by ever so slowly. Geoff's face dropped. He hadn't really expected her to agree to this. She was after all a very private person and it was ridiculously short notice. He started to say: 'OK fair enough. I understand...' 'Yes! I'll go. Why not?!' It felt good to do something really unplanned and unexpected and part of the thrill of that was shocking others, showing them a reckless side of her that they had never seen.

Geoff went to grab her hands to kiss them but found them to be tight little clenched balls. He sighed and swept his arms open in celebration. He didn't want to push his luck. And he couldn't believe his luck. He would really look after her, but didn't know how his parents – his mother in particular – was going to take to this idea of his to have a blind girlfriend. Not that he cared, but he knew that Alice, would. His girlfriend, a girl who was a friend, would need protection from any mind games that his mother might play. Oh yes, he knew his mum could be intimidating especially if it was someone encroaching on the affections of her only son.

He was aware that she had been a tad cold or otherwise indifferent (although he suspected it to be staged indifference) towards other girls he had introduced to her. He'd had a few girlfriends over the years, each one was nice but it hadn't worked out, they'd mutually broken things off. Still, it was as though no one could be good enough for her saintly son, and she thought his needs must be paramount in any kind of relationship he had, sometimes to the detriment of the girl. Mum was a problem. She would just have to be nice and make Alice's time with them as happy as possible. Alice was the 'one' for him – he felt it deep in his soul. He would be telling his parents that in due course. Alice had her pride and would hate to be the subject of the discussion on life mates.

Heck she probably doesn't even like me – at least not that way, he thought. Dad would be O.K, he always was, but mum, she wouldn't want anyone to hold up his progression in the world. Despite being a good woman, June Parker's son could see her become like a tigress protecting her young.

Geoff had always wanted to find someone he could serve and love and do things for, but his mother would see that as being a waste of his precious time, an albatross around his neck. He didn't really know if all of this was true or his own surmising of the situation with his mother. He had never had a frank talk with his mum. He did know he had possibly been spoilt for the girl of his dreams. He would certainly have to pick up his pyjamas and put wet towels out in the laundry. He would learn to cook and operate the washing machine – tough times demanded tough action!

There was no end to the things he would do for his loved one but he could almost hear Alice say 'If you wouldn't do it for your mother why would you do it for me?' He needed to be more responsible and that meant intercepting his mother before she did everything for him.

He knew that the Bible said the three most important things in life were faith, hope, and love and that the greatest of these was love. That would pave the way of his intentions for Alice. He would give her all the love she could ever want so that she could drop some of her defences and rest. He was starting to really love Alice and her blindness wasn't such a problem, in his eyes anyway. Geoff had to tell them about it. *I will tell them* he thought. Geoff was a dutiful son but would always defend Alice against any mean mother tactics.

'I'm just going to ring mum and dad while you pack' said Geoff taking out his mobile. 'Sure.' answered Alice, 'and while you're at it make sure you tell them I'm blind, won't you?'

'Sure, I will but I need to talk to them away from you. My parents aren't perfect you know and they may be a bit, well how would I put it?'

'Shocked' finished Alice. 'It's natural, I'm blind. How can they be happy about meeting your blind friend, who they'll probably assume as your new girlfriend? And by that I do mean your blind friend who is a girl.' she added quickly.

'I care what they think, and I won't stay if I'm the blind girl burden!' exclaimed Alice. 'You do have a way of dramatising this!' said Geoff. 'You're much more than a blind girl burden and you shouldn't say that! You are a beautiful, intelligent girl with a lot of wit. Don't ever think of yourself in a bad way.' Geoff smiled at her and went out in to the hall to make his call and Alice gave a coquettish little smirk at his sweetness.

Four

Alice bustled around getting ready for her holiday. She was twenty-eight, and she would be chaperoned by Geoff's parents. It was kind of funny. June would keep a hawk eye on them both, no doubt. It was her precious boy at stake here and she sensed from Geoff's tone that his mother had not been jumping out of her skin about her coming to stay. *She probably has a chastity belt for me to borrow while I'm there although I can't think of anything less likely to happen than needing that!*

'Leave her to me Alice, she's a marionette in my hands. Heck all I have to do is smile at her a certain way and give her a bit of cheek and she's eating out of my hand.'

'Fine,' said Alice thinking, *And I bet you get your sustenance eating off her table!* Somehow, work, her flat and everything seemed pretty unimportant and lifeless, not even worthy to be worried about. She left a message at work and smiled when she thought of the scandal she would cause not being there on Monday and in fact by being whisked off by a nice man. 'Half her luck' is what they would be thinking, perhaps a little mournfully as they carried on with the tedium of life.

The bush was drawing her back. She could almost smell the eucalyptus now but no, that was the eucalyptus oil that Geoff was using to get a mark off the door. How embarrassing! It wasn't as though she had toddlers drawing on her paintwork and she wondered how it had gotten there. She hadn't seen it obviously. She hoped upon hope that her nostrils would be clear at all times while she was with him and his parents. It would be too embarrassing if there was something *there*! How distracting would it be for them and how could they ever accept her if this was going to continually happen. It would try the patience of a saint. She would brush that aside figuratively and literally.

She gave a little giggle at her thoughts of disaster.

'What's that?' asked Geoff, as he rubbed the door with a cloth.

'Nothing you would be interested in I'm sure' smirked Alice. But then again, would you please tell me if there is anything hideous up my nose or on my clothing. You know without Jacquie or my friend the bus-driver Joe, you're the only one around who will be able to tell me.'

'You know Alice, you're the only girl who has ever asked me that.'

'You're just providing me with privileged information.' she giggled.

Her thoughts returned to the bush. With a daring sense of abandon her mind raced, as she took in the smells and sounds of the bush that lived in her memory. She decided to ring Jacquie. While she was meant to be packing in her room, she picked up her bedroom phone and dialled.

'So, you've finally gone bush...pig!' (Jacquie took teasing

seriously).

'You're really hilarious Jacquie!' said Alice sarcastically. She went on: 'It worries me a bit what everyone will think of me going away with a man, but Geoff has assured me that there would be no funny business. His parents will be chaperones for the next few days – probably to protect *his* honour.'

Jacquie laughed raucously down the phone. 'Now look who's being hilarious.' She said, teasing Alice's odd spinsterly ways.

'Who would want their son getting tied down with a blind girl? Any way, it doesn't really matter. Getting away to the bush will more than make up for the scandal rocking my insular world.'

'Just have fun.' said Jacquie fondly. 'And try to drop the dramatics.'

'But I don't deserve to have fun. I can't help but keep thinking that I'm betraying Stephen. That I should be dead with him...'

'Sure, but you can't have everything. You can't be dead *and* go to the bush with Geoff' 'You're so rude to me you know!' said Alice, wide awake to her friend's caustic comment.

'So, you think it's OK to have fun just for fun's sake?' asked Alice in desperation. 'Stop it Alice, you're making me tired. Look, just go and enjoy yourself and see what comes of it. No-one is asking you to marry the bloke – although you could do a lot worse. And *yes*, you do deserve this and *no* you haven't transgressed any major laws of morality or done anything to sully Stephen's memory. And don't corrupt that sweet country boy with your negativity.' Jacquie sighed as she finished talking. 'OK well gotta go. I'll tell work. When you know when you're coming back, let me know. I'll bring fresh milk over. Have a great time. Bye... love you.'

Alice fondly answered: 'Love you too.'

Jacquie had given her the go ahead and now she turned to her case and packed it with excitement and shakiness. She hoped Joe the bus driver wouldn't think any the worse of her going bush with a bloke. *Going away with Geoff, Geoff, more like half a bloke and half intelligent human being. Quite an enigma. Going away with him would be a bit like going away with Jacquie – a friend. But she's tougher on me and Geoff's softer.* Life was starting to get thrilling and she just couldn't wait to get going, even if she couldn't see where she was going.

Her heart leapt when she realised that she would be already gone before her work could give permission to go, not that they would have forbidden her to go. She felt a thrill at the spontaneity of it all, and yes, even at the slight irresponsibility. For Alice, irresponsibility was about the deadliest sin she could commit. It seemed like she was becoming her own alter ego, in that area. It seemed that everything she used to despise was suddenly becoming quite attractive to her. One thing was for sure and that being her total devotion to her old fiancée (she kept telling herself anyway) She was still hooked and had resigned herself to a life of blind spinsterhood. *Too much thinking.* She rummaged around packing stuff.

She went through her checklist: Tooth brush, check, toothpaste, a small one, (that should do for a while) check, plenty of undies, check, yes and a hairbrush, check. Good she thought and enough clothes to see her through at least a week. Mmmm, better pack more – what if it was two weeks? Best to be prepared she thought. Everything seemed to be there even herself, despite feeling as thought she could well float out through the window. She sat on the bed with excitement and with the satisfaction that she was leaving a tidy little flat with all repairs done to the door. That was thanks to Geoff's industrious handy man antics. That silly cat. He really messed up that door but not anymore. It was fixed just fine and all in good time!

Suddenly, she sat up off the bed. 'Tabby!' she exclaimed.

Geoff leapt to his feet and knocked on the bedroom door. 'What's the matter? Alice are you alright? The cat's out here. Tabby's out here and he's just eating his biscuits, he's fine.'

Alice strode across the room and opened the door.

'I can't go,' she said coldly.

What a change of tone. Now the ice maiden! Thought Geoff.

'Why not? You've packed, everything's under control and you know you need a holiday. No one's cares if you go away for a few days.'

'Look, it's not that, it's my cat,' she said curtly. 'How can I leave him here on his own? He's not used to strangers, so he would probably just run away if I go away. I just can't leave him. I know he's annoying but he would miss me too much. Don't you understand?' she said, annoying prickling tears brimming in her eyes, 'He's my best friend – he's always been here for me, and I can't leave him and that's that end of story.' Alice turned away feeling embarrassed by her outburst. 'I'm sorry…I don't mean to be so painful but this is what you would have had to put up with for however long we go away – me being painful.'

'A cat's a cat Alice, and it wouldn't care who fed it as long as someone did!' Instantly he regretted saying this because it made him seem totally heartless. Alice stiffened visibly and looked at his direction with a cold resolution about her. Ouch! She had certainly not liked that comment. On the farm the cats ate whatever they could find and were not sensitive about who bestowed affection on them. Not that they were mistreated.

They just weren't pampered, they were ratters. Geoff was helpless seeing Alice upset.

He knew he couldn't reason with her, as Tabby had been a part of her life for so long. He hit himself in the side of the head in exasperation. That didn't help. Just gave him a jolt and dull pain. A grim smile flitted across his face as he thought of suggesting he take the cat for a swim in the dam. No, definitely not a good idea to mention that joke, he decided.

Alice felt betrayed, betrayed by her loyalty to the cat and betrayed by Geoff's apparent callousness because one thing was for sure her first allegiance had to be the cat. Geoff was nice but her cat was her cat, horribly sensitive to other people although he didn't seem to mind Geoff. The last time she abandoned a loved one it had been Stephen on a godforsaken cliff, battered and killed.

Her cat had been the only one to give her comfort in the many lonely nights she had spent listening to the locomotion song of train diesel. She was not about to leave him at the mercy of other wicked territorial cats. Cat wounds from cat fights were notorious for becoming infected and abscessed. Then of course there were cruel people. She was certainly bound to her feline companion. She gave a deep sigh which almost deflated her whole body. She gently closed the door in Geoff's face, and started to unpack. She felt so disappointed. She really wanted to go, and resented Tabby at that moment.

Geoff knocked on the door. He put up with her rudeness, because she was so upset, but was starting to dislike the cat. He would have also liked to say that he could make nice tennis racket strings out of it, but decided against it. Alice's sense of humour did not include anything to do with that cat.

'We'll take him, Alice. Alice, we'll take Tabby with us!' She half opened the door. For a moment a look of joyful amazement caused her to cover her mouth with her hands and squealed with happiness. She was aware that she sounded like a pig but couldn't care less.

'Oh Geoff, Thank you. You are such a *good* person, not a cat lover but a really kind, nice person and *thank you!*' A big grin swept across her face, and she flung open the door. 'Really? *Really!* You don't mind bringing him. I don't have a cat cage but I do have a basket. I feel like such an idiot pressuring you into taking my cat of all things, on holidays. Cats aren't good travellers you know.'

'I know' acknowledged Geoff, 'At least they don't hang their heads out of a window. 'Last week I was driving behind a car that had an Alsatian sticking its head out of the window. It coughed and a huge transparent film of vomit (it may have been mucous) sailed out. None got on my car.'

Alice laughed out loud, and shivered with horror at the story and secretly hoped that her cat wouldn't do the same thing. If he ever got his head out of the car, she felt sure that the rest of him would squeeze through like toothpaste. In this life, with cats there were no guarantees. Geoff could be funny at times and she liked his dog anecdote. 'The cat will settle in well on the farm as long and as it doesn't go near the dogs. We supplement their diet with cats when we can.' he added smiling then instantly regretted antagonizing her even in fun because the cat's welfare was something she didn't take lightly. 'Don't worry, the dogs don't normally go for cats because they're well fed,' laughed Geoff.

Alice laughed but her face went pale when she thought of a whole lot of aggressive, fast cattle dogs.

'Do you mean that?!' she croaked.

'Don't worry, I'm being silly Alice. The cats and dogs get on well. There is sort of truce between them and if anything, the cats rule on the farm and the dogs toe the line.' 'You mean they all get on?' said Alice relieved.

Alice frowned and Geoff prepared for another outburst from her when she gave an unsuccessfully suppressed snigger. 'You really are a bush pig!' she smiled.

'Feral actually.' said Geoff. 'Jacquie says I am, and she would know.

'Feral and feculent!' giggled Alice. 'She called me one too.'

'I'll need the dictionary for that one.' smiled Geoff. Although he did understand her – he wasn't a complete uneducated dummy. He also knew Alice had girly confidential conversations with Jacquie. He could only guess at the things they discussed.

'All I ask is what any friend would ask being that their friend be considered when plans were made with another friend.' said Alice.

'By friend you mean cat?' Geoff's mouth kinked up on one side.

'Yep, cat, feline' Alice smiled.

'With claws and sharp teeth'

'A soft furry pet!' Alice said reassuringly.

'We'll see when we're on the road how harmless he is. For all I know he might run amuck inside the car scratching the buggery out of the leather.'

'Leather?' smiled Alice, shaping the word luxuriously.

'Don't make me apologise for my good taste. A little bit of leather makes all the hard work worthwhile.'

Alice relented and started to pack her things again.

Geoff shook his head and sighed in relief and thought to himself this could take forever.

'Geoff, how do I know that you are really safe, you know, to be with?'

'Well, *our* friend Jacquie likes me, *and* I have nice parents, *and* hang dang it, I'm taking a cat on holidays. I would have thought that alone would be proof enough!' said Geoff with mock indignation.

'Yes, you do have a point. Not many men would put up with that, a cat in the car, I mean one apart from me.' she laughed.

'Oh, you're just a kitten and you don't have any claws.' said Geoff.

'You underestimate me sir,' said Alice sounding like a heroine from a Jane Austen story.

Geoff raised his eyebrows quizzically.

Geoff loaded her cases into the four-wheel drive, and last of all, Tabby in his little cane picnic basket, with folding in lid was placed in the middle of the front seat. He gave a low growl that sent chills up Geoff's spine. When it comes to hideous nocturnal sound, cats were only to be outdone by koalas and possums. This cat was voicing his misery in the picnic basket in broad daylight.

Alice spoke reassuringly. 'Calm down Tabby, just be a good boy now.' The cat had a wild-eyed look of dread but to its credit didn't bite her hand as she stroked him.

'I don't think you can reason with him.' said Geoff sagely, a real cat expert.

'You're lucky he isn't biting the hand that feeds him.'

'But he would probably bite the hand of anyone else that fed him. You see Tabby and I have a lot in common.'

'Such as?' asked Geoff.

'We're quite private people (Tabby and I) but we are affectionate to people we give our allegiance to, providing...'

'Providing?' enquired Geoff, amused.

'Providing those people don't let us down.'

'And what would 'other' people do that would let you down?'

'I don't actually know until it happens.'

Great! thought Geoff. *She's more cryptic than a crossword.*

He burst out laughing and shook his head, and glanced over at the basket. The cat sounded eery and his tiny tenacious talons clung to the side of the high basket as Alice held the lid down firmly. She pulled his paws away from the edge of the basket and closed the lid. She marvelled that his wire hard tendons didn't snap.

'If you let go of him, he'll be gone,' chuckled Geoff and then in a mystic voice, added 'never to be seen again!'

'Well, you may well laugh, but he's really terrified and I don't know how he'll cope with all this.'

'And I can state *cat*egorically that he will.' said Geoff with an impish smile.

'Look!' exclaimed Alice in exasperation, 'You don't know my cat, and don't pretend you do.'

'Fine.' said Geoff letting her comment pass over his head. Once they had strapped their seatbelts on, and the four-wheel drive turned over and lurched forward. Soon they had joined the painfully slow exodus of traffic from the city.

Alice thought, *I can't believe it. Here I am going on a holiday with someone I've only known a week or two. What is wrong with me? He does seem trustworthy, and he makes me laugh…. a laughing axe murderer. Great! I wonder what work will think when I don't turn up on Monday.* A twinge of fear passed through her that she was going to enjoy herself. *Everyone says I should have fun, but I haven't had fun for so long that the thought of a holiday makes me feel guilty because someone is missing and that's Stephen. In a way he will be coming on the holiday with me. There is so much in my life that I haven't told Geoff and maybe I never will.* With shame she thought that she had not shared her faith with him, the faith that had in the past been so vital to her existence. *So much sad bad stuff has happened. I'm a poor example of a follower of Jesus. Where is my joy in life, my stoicism, my kindness? Jacquie knows I'm a believer but we never talk about it as it causes fights (how ironic when I should be a peacemaker).* Alice knew what she should believe but the guilt and shame had brought her down and had made her frequently judgmental of others. *If I can't allow myself any happiness, all the laughing people seem wanton and frivolous. How amusing that I would think non-Christians to be lost when I am in a wilderness of my own making. Now,* she thought, *should I tell Geoff any of that? No way! A bit of discretion needed here, I think. To protect myself of course.*

As the car hummed along the highway, Alice prayed silently. *You see God, I have pretty much fallen by the wayside. It's not because I don't love you (I do) but I'm too scared of you. The rules are too hard to follow. I won't read the bible while we're away but I will pray (I always do). Hopefully I can get to the stage where I'm successful and confident the way I used to be. Then I will feel I am more worthy of having you in my life. Going away with a stranger who may or may not share my faith in you is I suppose a travesty but please forgive me for this. I'm so looking forward to it.*

I know, I know, I will talk to him sometime about you – just not now. He's driving and trying to get us out of the city in one piece. And this Cat is near to exploding point – hopefully not at his tail end.

Now her main duty was to keep the cat under control. The thought of it rampaging around in the vehicle raking the leather with its rose-thorn claws, was a truly chilling thought. *Just hold that thought and don't let it happen!*

Oh, for heaven's sake girl drop the doom and gloom and just have fun!

Alice was soaking in the rhythm of the road – the sound of rubber on ash felt, a smooth rumbly, comforting noise. After a little while she nodded off, but not before tying the basket's escape end shut. A samurai cat whooshing all around just would not do.

Five

Cars tooted, and the exhaust fumes filled the air. They had reached a bank up. Geoff sighed and Alice could hear him tapping his fingers on the steering wheel impatiently. Alice felt sorry for him and said 'Don't worry, we'll get through…eventually. Your sighs are changing the air pressure in here. Negative ions – that's what it is and they might affect the cat.' she joked, trying to lighten the mood.

'What on earth are you talking about? I've never heard of sighing making negative ions.

You made that up, didn't you?'

'Maybe,' said Alice with slight smile. 'But it might be true.'

'Alice, for one who seems so deceptively truthful and a yes a bit prim, you can really spin whopper.' said Geoff.

'Mmm, I must be bored. I usually do that sort of thing when I'm bored. Perhaps we should talk but maybe we shouldn't because you're driving and have to concentrate.' said Alice sagely.

'As soon as we get out of here, I promise we can talk. In fact, I'll look forward to it. Is that OK?

Alice settled deeper in her seat with a self-satisfied grin – which she forgot to hide.

Geoff noticed, and was pleased – she wanted to talk to him!

Tabby yowled relentlessly which was really getting to Geoff, but he thought about the bigger picture, which was a happy Alice coming on holiday with him, so anything this cat could dish up was worth it. He made that decision right from the time he suggested taking the cat with them. It was just as well that Alice could not see the long line of cars that wound up the hill and no doubt over the other side and beyond. Every second Suburbanite had left Melbourne tonight to live it up either at the beach or in the mountains. *The beach at this time of the year, Autumn, would be starting to get chilly. But then again so would the mountains. One thing was certain. There will be quite a frost tomorrow morning and maybe some snow on the ranges. The cattle will be arriving at dad's property soon. They would have to go to higher ground.* Geoff thought to himself, *I wonder why I always think to myself. I could tell Alice all of this. It's just that I'm not used to talking to someone in the land cruiser. Women talk more than men it seems to me. I guess I just assume she wouldn't be interested.* Testing the waters, he said:

'Looks like a frost tomorrow morning.' said Geoff.

'And probably a bit of snow in the highlands,' answered Alice. She continued: 'It said on the news that it's raining in the high country. Does that mean that there will be flooding at your parent's farm?'

'Yes possibly.' he replied.

'What about your cows? Will it affect them? Will it flood with all the rain coming from higher up?'

How uncanny, Geoff thought. *She is on my wave length. All I have to do is talk and listen, just as if she were my best mate.* And *she's cute. Mmmm. What a lucky bloke am I.*

They kept up a comfortable conversation and Geoff wished she could see the sight now as they were getting to the freeway where there was bush all around as well as farm land. Alice was nervous. Tabby was terrified, and consistent with his protests. 'Your cat really does hate being in the car. He's probably never been in one before except to sneak in through an open window at night and wee in it – as they do.' 'Excuse me, Geoff, other cats may do disgusting things like that but Tabby wouldn't dream of it.' She pulled the basket closer against her and sniffed.

'Oh really!?' teased Geoff. 'He wouldn't sneak into a car and mark his territory? Well, he's got class Alice, probably because of his owner!'

'Naturally.' smiled Alice. 'And by the way he's desexed, so he doesn't go in for all those macho cat antics now.'

'He's retired then from the tomcat hood,' said Geoff 'just a stay-at-home drop hair on the cushion kinda cat.'

'Yes, actually but now he's all stirred up and he won't settle down. Babies who are crazy with tiredness get taken for drives by their crazy sleep deprived parents to lull them off to sleep. Some cats are like that in cars.' her voice trailed off.

'But not Tabby,' said Geoff.

'Not Tabby. By the way are we out of the city?'

'Yep, well and truly.' said Geoff. 'I think every one's gone to the coast and so the road is really quiet, so you see we can talk. In fact, it would be good. It'll keep me awake.'

'No, you talk Geoff.'

'Well,' he sighed as he started a story. 'This is about a cat so you will probably like it. It's really quite sad, a case of 'pet favoured over children abuse', and the worst I've heard.'

Alice looked shocked, but Geoff reassured her 'It's nothing to worry about – kind of funny. You may get a giggle out of it. It's a true story, OK?'

'Shelby was staying at her grandmother's house…'

'Wait, who's Shelby?' asked Alice.

'Oh, well she was a good friend from years ago.'

'Oh.' Said Alice, full of meaning.

'Well, we did go out for a few months, but no mainly we're just friends.'

'Do you see her much now?' Alice asked, not believing how nosy she was being. 'Well not much now. She's married and living in Brisbane, I think. Anyway, do you want to hear the story or not? It's to do with a cat.'

'Ok.'

Why would she care about one of my old girlfriends? Geoff wondered. He recollected his thoughts, and began the story again.

'So…Shelby would stay with her parents at her grandmother's home in the country. A Tabby Point Siamese used to visit, and Shelby's father tried to deter it by throwing water on it.' Alice made a face, but didn't comment. She hated cruelty to animals – her own cat hurling moments included.

Geoff continued. 'When he found out that it was a special breed (a Siamese), and not just a common cat, and that it probably had a pedigree, he got a bit interested in it and started to coax it back. In the end, it became his mother's closest companion and left untold tons of white hair all through the house causing allergies for many years to come. When Shelby's grandmother died her father took the cat to live in the city with him.'

'Yes and?' said Alice keen to hear the punch line of the story it if indeed there was one.

'Well, my friend...' Geoff continued.

'Shelby.' interjected Alice.

'Yes, that's right continued Geoff. 'She hated the cat because even though it was timid and wary of strangers it would arch its bony little hind end up against her dad's hand so he could scratch its back and he trained it to roll over saying like an indulgent parent. (To the cat!): 'Rolleeover. Come on little darling rolleeover, that's a little girl'. You see that was where the problem, started, with the terms of endearment that were so forthcoming when the cat was around. If it got a fright and hid under a bed Shelby's dad would croon: 'Come on out little girl. Are you hungry little girl? Come on out sweetheart.' Shelby and her sisters all hated the cat, and one day my friend said to her father: 'Dad, that cat gets the affection and terms of endearment that we never got.' He thought they were being ridiculous.

'Yep, they were in their rights to say that to him.' agreed Alice. 'I can honestly say that I too have never had any sweet talk, apart from yours of course Geoff.' She said, as a half joke, half shameless flirt. *Why did I blurt that out? I don't want to give him the wrong idea – surely, he knows I'm just joking!*

'Really? My darling girl I can't believe that!' he laughed. Alice smiled, then blushed despite herself.

Suddenly there was silence, and then she said 'I love it when people speak sweet and kind words to me! Don't you think most people do?'

'Well,' said Geoff 'My mum has always called me embarrassing things. Darling, sweetheart precious you name it she had no shame!' He laughed as he remembered something else:

'Once I was playing footy and at half time, mum came out, inspected my grazed knee and gave me a big cuddle (I was eighteen!). It was so embarrassing that when I was older, I would never tell her where I was umpiring – I umpired Aussie Rules – because I couldn't be sure she wouldn't do it again.'

'Ooh,' said Alice laughed heartily at the vision of a great big eighteen-year-old fending off a love sick mother. It was hilarious!

'My dad is not much better.' Geoff went on. 'Sure, he seems a bit of the 'gruff macho' type, but he's been so over-the-top affectionate. From when I was little, he would cuddle me, play fight, kiss me – this is the funny part – nearly every morning before he'd go out to work on the farm, he'd jump into bed with me! Give me a big smooch and wake me up. Well, he kind of forgot that I grew up past being a toddler, you know? Even just before I went to live in the city for Uni (when I was 18) he'd still jump into bed with me in the morning! – to annoy me more than anything. So, embarrassing.' Geoff smiled as he told these stories, Alice could tell that he secretly loved being the object of his parent's adoration.

'It makes me feel grateful for my lack of affection. It must have been tough on you to be over-dosed with affection and in front of your friends, yes that would be unforgettable and maybe unforgiveable...Say does your dad still jump into bed with you?'

Geoff laughed 'No – not for about ten years, but I wouldn't put it past him!' Geoff tapped the steering wheel. They sat, for a big wait, where the road was being fixed. The cat started his ever-hopeful bid for freedom, scrabbling and scratching the sides of the basket – keeping up the noise just so they hadn't forgotten that he was unhappy. Geoff decided that he would never have a picnic out of that picnic basket.

After what seemed like several hours, but which was actually only more like fifteen minutes, the traffic sped up and they were suddenly on the freeway, again cruising with bushland on either side.

Another hour went by and Alice was starting to nod off. Geoff drove on into the afternoon. By about 3 o'clock he said gently and giving her shoulder a little shake: 'Alice we're coming to a turn off. Would you like to meet my Aunty Linda and Uncle Reg? They live up this way.' Alice nodded, sleepily. Tabby howled, mournfully with eyes like saucers. *Honestly* thought Geoff *you would think he had just seen the hound of Baskervilles. Out on the moor being hunted down by dog the size of a pony. It was just a car ride. What was the drama?* He was glad he had the basket tied up so there was only a glimpse of the cat's nose. He was keen to get out of the car for a while and see his favourite Aunt and Uncle. They always thought the best of him and maybe that was why he liked them so much because they liked him. It made him want to be good. The weather was pretty squally and he knew it had been raining up in the mountains. The four-wheel drive wound around a narrow steep road with tall eucalypts on either side. Strings and sheets of bark were in the process of coming off them – crackly to crunch underfoot but smooth and almost powdery to the touch. The smell found its way inside the car as Geoff wound down his window an inch. Alice loved that smell and she started to spark up after her nap. The road became increasingly windy and the cat was like an eel almost knotting itself in panic. The wild eucalypt air was making him wild. Alice thought about it. It could be that or it could be something else. She had figured it out and then hesitantly spoke. It was something that had to be said.

'Geoff, I think Tabby wants to go to the toilet'

'What? Right here right now right here right here right now?' he imitated a popular song that was being played a lot on the radio although not at the same time. 'He's picked a fine time. It's too narrow to stop here. We'll have to stop up at the lookout up ahead. He shook his head as he stopped on the side of the road.

'Are you angry?' asked Alice. 'I mean he had to go, and you know the old saying, when you've got to go you've got to go.'

'Put it this way, I'd rather he went out there than in here, and darling girl, how could I be angry with you, honestly?' he teased, hoping to make her blush again.

Alice gave a tentative crooked smile and carefully opened the lid and lifted Tabby out of the basket.

'Okay mate, go to it,' said Geoff. The cat didn't need any encouragement. With one soulful look at Alice, he took off and bounded into the scrub.

'Is he going?' asked Alice.

Geoff shook his head in disgust and looked to the sky in despair, as if hoping for divine intervention.

'Going, yes he's going.' murmured Geoff as the cat disappeared from view having melted into the thick scrub.

When she heard the crashing of bark and bracken made by Geoff, Alice guessed what had happened. The cat was answering the call of the wild. She covered her mouth and gasped inwardly, feeling her heart shrink as if cold hands had grabbed it, but she didn't say anything knowing how terrified Geoff must be feeling now Geoff leapt down the side of the embankment and great clods of dirt plumped after him. Tabby was not to be seen and Geoff couldn't even remember feeling such dread. This girl who he, well, let's not beat around the bush, yes loved, would cast him off if this wretched cat was lost. He crashed through the undergrowth and was scratched by bracken and tea tree bushes.

'Tabby, Tabby,' pleaded Alice. 'Please come back. We'll have a great holiday. Come out, come back, please.' *Lord as usual I'm here praying for something. I know I don't deserve it but could you please bring Tabby back. I need him.*

'Look he'll come back we'll just have to wait.' said Geoff, not believing this for a moment, but hoping it was true.

Nearly an hour passed and Alice and Geoff sat side by side on the embankment. The happy trickle of a small stream seemed to do its best to soothe them as did the haunting bellbird's song, which rang intermittently through the quiet eucalypt forest. The smell of damp moss and fragrant herbs made the scene complete and should have been completely relaxing except for the crisis they were in. Geoff had nothing to say, just thought it wise to not to get into a conversation that could escalate into hysteria and the very real prospect of it all ending in tears! *I hope that stupid cat comes back soon.*

If it wasn't such a silent vigil, they probably would have enjoyed this and been able to talk, but all had to be silent so that the cat would come into the open.

Suddenly Geoff hissed. 'I see him Alice, I see the blighter.' He strained to see and sure enough, a very subtle, tabby shadow was creeping along the gully side, quite close to them.

Alice wasn't sure she liked her cat being called a 'blighter'.

'Pass the blanket please.' he whispered. Alice handed it to him.

A dancing blue wren mesmerised Tabby, and Geoff crept up imperceptibly until he was only metres away from the stalking cat. Tabby ignored Geoff being totally absorbed by this intriguing bobbing hopping little blue jewel. Tabby's tail flicked at the end like a snake. Geoff threw the blanket over the cat like a seasoned gladiator throwing a net over his victim. Tabby was really angry. He let out a yowl of indignation, rage and disappointment. That wren would have made him feel like a real cat. A hunter! Geoff had some raked bloody marks on his arm and a puncture from the monster's teeth on the top of his hand. How could anyone be a vet? However worse than the injuries sustained would have been if the cat had gone AWOL for good.

Now back in the loathsome car, Tabby flattened out in his basket. No amount of reassurance from Alice could stop his horrid growling. Not only had he been done out of his freedom, he'd been done out of dinner and a sense of cat-hood.

'Look,' reasoned Alice to the cat, 'you wouldn't have enjoyed that bird. It was all feathers and bones. When we get to Geoff's Aunty's place, you can have some Kitty Queen, with extra pilchards! Yum, Yum.'

Geoff gave a queasy smile and turned the wheel around down the gravelly road after spotting the sign 'Blue Gum Brook'. It was Aunty Linda and Uncle Reg's farm. The house was a white weatherboard with a tin roof. It sat on a gentle rise that would drain well in the rain. A couple of black kelpies ran out to greet them, barking, jumping and slobbering as Geoff fended them off, keen to protect Alice and the cat from their rampant enthusiasm. 'Try to ignore them, they're just saying hello.'

'Hello.' said Alice hesitantly holding the basket up and holding the lid down at the same time – not an easy task.

'Here I'll carry that.' said Geoff, swooping the basket from her.

'Thanks Geoff 'They're real dogs, aren't they? Full of beans.'

'Yep', agreed Geoff, 'only real dogs here.'

Alice took his arm, feeling embarrassed that she needed leading. The cat's arm thrust up through the flaps of the baskets fully stretched, sinuous and strong *and* fully equipped with hooks.

From the kitchen window Aunty Linda saw them. She wiped her hands on a tea towel and exclaimed to her Reg:

'Look whose here! It's Geoff with a little friend and I think they've bought a picnic basket for us. How thoughtful, but then again Geoff is a considerate boy.'

'Yes, but not that considerate. I don't like your chances of that basket having a picnic in it.'

'Oh Reg.' was all said Linda straightening her apron and her hair.

'Just realistic luv.' said Reg peering out of the kitchen window. 'He usually lobs over and eats us out of house and home. I'll just put those cows and calves in the safe paddock and I'll be back in a few minutes. Leave a scone for me luv.'

'Yes, yes of course Reg. Don't be long.'

The kelpies were beside themselves with excitement. Like their owners the dogs regarded strangers as a very welcome addition to the day. They didn't know how to be aggressive, just overwhelming in their welcoming.

Six

Aunty Linda smiled radiantly; her lined face full of warmth as her fine well-loved nephew walked through the gate down to the path to the house. Geoff wished that Alice could see the flowers blooming at this time of the year.

The Japanese wind flowers with their large velvety, daisy blooms nodded in the breeze, and the daphnia delicate and bejewelled didn't escape Alice's sensitive nostrils.

'Oh, Daphnia! It smells heavenly!'

'Yes, it surely is my dear, at its fragrant best!' said Linda taking Alice's hand. 'I'm Linda, Geoff's Aunty.'

'Best Aunty!' said Geoff popping a kiss on her cheek. 'Yes, Geoff you are wonderful but I am just being introduced to this darling girl.'

'Alice' said Alice. 'Yes, Alice how are you darling? Did you have a good trip? He *should* have told me you were coming! Luckily I made some scones.' she said enfolding Alice with her affectionate and large arm.

'You always make scones!' said Geoff.

'It just seems like I do,' said Aunty Linda with a little sigh.

'I hope you train this boy to not expect scones whenever he feels like them!' 'I'm afraid I'm not one to train anyone because

I am so imperfect myself – although I must say I made biscuits for him when he fixed the scratches on my laundry door that the cat made.'

'Aunty Linda,' said Geoff, 'Give the girl a chance to speak (and don't encourage her to say nasty things about me!) This is Alice all the way from the big city!'

'I hope you like it up here Alice, but excuse me for being nosy but I gather that your basket isn't full of bread, cheese, and wine!'

The cat was yowling and Geoff was suddenly aware of his charge and the importance of it in the whole scenario. No cat, no holiday with Alice.

Alice bunched up her face and shook her head. 'Sorry, there's no gourmet food in here. I didn't know we were coming here otherwise I would have…'

'Would have? No would haves here. I have everything we need here and you my captive guests. It's a good chance for me to make you something nice for afternoon tea.' Linda giggled. 'Reg pines for human company because he reckons, I don't bother cooking anything special unless we have guests and I guess that is true.' Linda giggled again and said 'Bring kitty in, and I'll give him some milk after his stomach has settled from that twisty road.'

Alice relaxed once they were inside the house. At least Tabby couldn't run off very far now but as she took him out of the basket, he looked very furtive.

'We've had plenty of rain, and Reg's been bringing the beasts up to higher ground now that the creek's rising.' said Linda.

'Most will make their way up but some are dumber than others and need that little prod, cattle prod so to speak.' she laughed. 'Of course, we don't use electric cattle prods out here in the bush, just a stick of a tree actually.' Her jokes about the cattle prod were lost on Alice who had no knowledge of bush practices. 'Aunty Linda,' said Alice with embarrassment in her voice. She thought she would get it out in the open right away. 'I'm blind.'

'I know dear.' Aunty Linda patted her hand and gave it a squeeze, and no more was said though her eyes became instantly watery. Uncle Reg had just finished settling the cows and calves in a safe paddock away from the rising waters and came noisily stumping into the back wooden verandah in what Alice thought were the loudest gumboots she had ever heard.

He burst through the door, and with a big smile grabbed Geoff's hand. 'Gidday mate!' he said slapping his other hand down on Geoff's back.

'It's good to see you. You shouldn't be such a stranger! You know you're Aunty only cooks when we have people over, so come more often!'

'How can you say that Reg?' said Linda. 'This morning you had scrambled eggs, lunch was fresh grilled trout, and dinner is going to be lambs fry and bacon.'

'And onion!' laughed Reg.

'Yes, and onion! And other veg which you should have more of.' said Linda.

His Uncle looked a little sheepish and changed the subject

saying: 'The rain is good but the creeks are rising.' Then glancing around he saw Alice.

Then turning to Geoff, he exclaimed: '*You're* a dark horse not telling us about your girlfriend!' Reg wasn't trying to embarrass Geoff and Alice but he did. He was simply stating what he thought was the obvious.

'This is my friend Alice,' said Geoff.

'Nice to meet you love!' said Reg, who was always overjoyed to see Geoff and especially honoured to meet his girlfriend, and a pretty one at that! Linda raised her eyebrows at Reg. He got the hint and didn't say girlfriend again but it was on the tip of his tongue and he had to keep at least one brain cell connected to his tongue so he wouldn't comment on Geoff's new girlfriend again.

Linda took him aside in the kitchen, and told him about Alice's handicap and he was especially sweet and gentle towards her afterwards which Alice felt was perhaps worse than if he had been openly shocked by her blindness. He was very attentive towards her in the biscuit and scone department, offering her food time and time again even commenting that she was little on the thin side. Alice was touched.

'Sometimes having to eat is a real chore and a real bore. I don't know why. You know it's the smell of food that totally wins me over.'

'It could be worse' said Reg. 'You could eat like a horse and end up like me, or us, the extra one of me there is now!'

Alice laughed 'I'm sure you burn most of it up looking after the farm.' she said diplomatically.

Reg slapped his tummy loudly saying that his mates were wondering when it's due. 'I'm not like this young fella here who runs and plays sport and goes to the 'gym' (He said gym sneeringly).

'In leotards?!' laughed Linda.

'Of course not.' Geoff grinned and shook his head.

'Well, you wouldn't get me wearing such an outfit.' said Reg.

'And I'm glad of it!' exclaimed Geoff.

'Well, the rain has stopped for the time being but it's probably still raining further up. They reckon the creek'll peak tomorrow morning. I'll bring the rest of the beasts to high ground before then.'

'Do you need any help?' asked Geoff.

'No, it's all under control. I only have to bring twenty from the frontage up to the paddocks above the road. Not a big job. Your dad has a lot more to bring up to higher ground.'

Geoff nodded. 'Yeh and the ones I got at the sale as well.'

'Good cattle?' asked Reg.

'Nice breeders and a few yearlings to fatten up. The market's pretty good at the moment.'

'The big rectangular cows are the secret,' said Reg. 'No trouble calving and they throw a good type of calf. My cattle are good but your dad's are better.'

'I wouldn't say that.' said Geoff who was interested but thinking it was time to get moving. They still had a way to go.

Alice found this conversation much more interesting than town talk of striking bus drivers, traffic pile ups, and the efforts everyone seemed to take to stay 'in shape.'

'Do you like Melbourne dear?' said Aunty Linda handing Alice a cup of tea.

'For a busy city it's not too bad, but I sure do miss the bush. I didn't know how much I missed it until I got here. The smells are thrilling and bring back memories. The eucalypts and just the smell of running water, you know down on the bank.'

'Why dear, how expressive you are. You should write some of that down. It's lovely and it gave me goose pimples.'

'Really!' smiled Alice, 'thank you for that little compliment. I will treasure it.' 'I'm full of compliments today. I think I excelled with my scones today and that makes me happy.' said Linda beaming.

'Well, I would have to agree,' said Alice. 'Actually, they were the nicest ones I have had in living memory!'

Linda burst into a loud shrieking giggle and squeezed Alice's hand yet again.

Geoff looked and then frowned. They really had to get going. Time was getting away.

They said their goodbyes. 'If you ever need anything just ring.' said Linda.

'We're only a phone call away you know!' added Reg.

'I do appreciate that very much'. said Alice touched by their concern.

There was an awkward silence then the tension eased when Tabby vomited on the floor near the old wood stove. Alice heard the cough then the dry wretch, a sound she recognized from Tabby's fur ball episodes.

'Don't worry dear, I'll fix it.' said Linda.

'I'm so sorry,' said Alice. 'I hope it wasn't on a rug.'

'That's something not to be found in this kitchen.' said Linda knowingly.

Aunty Linda was a staunch country girl, and poddy calves in the kitchen had caused her much grief when she used to have nice decorative rugs on the floor – more trouble than this queasy cat in fact. Reg would sometimes still bring in a weak calf in that needed warmth and special care. They often had scour.

'He'll be alright now that he has gotten rid of that.' said Linda confidently.

After yet one more cup of tea they were on their way. They waved (especially Alice) until Geoff's Aunt and Uncle had disappeared from view, and Alice felt genuine sadness at having to leave such a warm fold.

On the road again Geoff was keen to discuss his beloved Aunt and Uncle. 'I'm fond of Aunty Linda but she *does* divide the day up into one long tea drinking binge. There's always been breakfast, then morning tea, lunch, afternoon tea, dinner and then supper, all involving tea.

'Ever since I've been a little boy, I've never known a time when her biscuit barrel was empty. She makes the most fantastic ginger fluff sponges in the world – all in her old wood stove. Yes, she's amazing. But Alice *your* biscuits really did take the cake… because it was *you* who made them!'

'Don't you think that's a bit patronizing Geoff, to like my biscuits just because I made them!' but she smiled as she said this. Then she really got going. 'Heck, anyone can cook. All you need is a recipe, and to be able to read, follow the instructions and voila it's done. I know that my biscuits were not spectacular and I'm not sensitive on the issue so please don't feel you have to rave about them.'

Geoff smiled at her with kind eyes. Yes, he had said a rather stupid thing and he knew it. He had walked into the biscuit battle field like a regular ginger bread man to the picnic.

He rambled on and Alice listened. After all it was something of a phenomenon when a man actually talked and showed his emotions and even more so when he talked about biscuits and the making of them. She was especially intrigued as he went on to discuss his uncle. He continued: 'Uncle Reg is a hard worker with not a malicious streak in him. It takes a lot of cooking to fill up his hollow legs. He only has a bit of a paunch on him for a man his age.'

'Hmm…,' said Alice. 'I thought it seemed like he ate about ten scones with raspberry jam and cream.'

'Yes, that would be about right.' said Geoff chuckling.

'And I notice that food features hugely in the country vernacular.'

'No more than anywhere else.' said Geoff starting to take the subject seriously and to heart.

'You know what I think?'

'What?' asked Geoff with interest.

'I think the simple life in the country is the best, and I would be honoured if a man ate ten of my fictional scones – but he could lose his teeth in them. There's the tragedy.'

Geoff thought this was funny, Alice was pleased that she could make him laugh.

On they went through the bush along the winding unsealed road. It was loud, grinding and hypnotic. They had tied the top of the picnic basket down again so Tabby had to accept his incarceration a bit longer. Geoff smiled that he was driving along with his precious Alice. Yes, he did regard her as his and as such he wanted to shower her with as much love and care that he could. As he drove into the sunset, the rosy fire flooded sky filled him with a fullness and joy.

Thank Lord for this. It's all so peaceful now. Please let Alice have a lovely time up at the farm. Actually, let us both recharge, and dare I ask but could she get fond of me, not just for all the cat related heroics I've been responsible for lately.

Seven

Alice rubbed her eyes as the four-wheel drive rumbled through the gate of Geoff's parent's farm.

She sensed the night was closing in, and it was. The car headlights made tunnels of light in the darkness and they skimmed over grass, fences and the glowing eyes of mildly interested cattle.

Alice smiled as she heard the vehicle roll to a stop. She gave a yawn and stretch as did the cat which had finally been lulled to sleep by the road.

Geoff opened the car door and a cold breath of Autumn hit him. He wasn't impressed. *It's not meant to be Winter yet. I hope it won't be like this while Alice is here but it is mountain country. It could even snow knowing my luck.*

There were more voices and the sound of feet crunching down a gravel path.

Alice felt a little stupid standing there, holding her cat in its basket.

'So, this is Alice.' came a voice that sounded kind but with a hint of caution – his mother.

'I'm June, Alice.'

'It's lovely to meet you June,' Alice said, as June gave her a welcome kiss on the cheek. Alice clasped her hand but noticed that, or may be imagined that the grip did not hold the warmth and welcome that her sister Linda had.

'Did you have a good trip?'

'Yes, we did, apart from the…did Geoff tell you about my cat?' said Alice nervously. 'Well, no, dear. Not to worry. The cat can stay in the wash house.'

'I brought his litter tray', added Alice hoping to sound helpful.

'Good girl,' said June 'but let's get out of this freezing air!'

'Mayyyyyyte!' said a warm deep voice – which sounded uncannily like Geoff's voice – but a bit more gravelly. He gave his son a big bear hug like he hadn't seen him in years – it had only been a week.

'Hi Dad.' said Geoff. 'This is Alice, who I told you about.'

'Hello Mr Parker, pleased to meet you.' said Alice nervously.

Geoff's Dad grasped Alice's hand warmly, saying 'Call me Al, it's easy to remember.

You know, Parker, Al Packer', like a long-necked sheep?'

'Oh, an Alpaca!' Alice gave a little chuckle. She had so much nervous energy coursing through her that Mr Parker's little joke seemed funnier than it normally would, and June shushed him in the background. Geoff was standing up for his dad. 'Mum, dad's got to practice his stand-up comedy on someone!'

'But why here and why now and why poor Alice?' came Junes exasperated voice.

'You're just privileged my dear.' came Al Parker's reply directed at Alice.

'I most certainly am,' said Alice laughing.

There was a snort that Alice guessed to be from June. Yes, Al Packer's jokes were a little on the unfunny, desperate side but she figured that the two of them had been living in the bush a long time, perhaps too long.

'Yep, let's go in.' said Allen – who Alice was determined she would call Al. Already,

Alice was getting a picture of the dynamics in this family and she decided it was more matriarchal than anything else. *June could do with a laugh* she thought.

'Al!' snapped June, 'Don't keep the poor girl out in the cold.' She didn't find his ridiculous comments about Alpacas funny and wished he would grow up. Once inside June buzzed around in the kitchen getting warm drinks for every one which she enjoyed doing but was offended that this young lass wouldn't join her in the domestic fun. Alice felt sure that June would have her best china out and deliberately decided not the help in the kitchen, feeling that she could well become a proverbial bull in a china shop or actually a heifer since she was female. June just didn't understand that even though Alice was blind she was bound by the etiquette of the bush to at least look helpful in the hostess's home. Alice was quite comfortable talking with her husband and son by a crackling fire while she (the work horse as she saw it) slaved away to please everyone. Her mind was ticking over.

When I met Al's parents, I at least tried to make a good impression! Maybe she's liberated and doesn't believe in waiting on men which is fair

enough I suppose. It's the done thing around here and it doesn't worry me because I've done it so long and I would go without food myself to make sure the men are fed. I've gone without steak so they wouldn't miss out.

I'll give her the benefit of the doubt. I mean she is blind of course, the poor thing. And being from the city, she probably doesn't know our way of doing things. I suppose I should be glad that she is so relaxed here that she doesn't feel the need to leap up every two seconds the way I do – have to do!

Alice was quite oblivious to this current of ill feeling that she was inadvertently causing and happily sipped her hot chocolate soaking in the warmth of the fizzing spitting fire as moisture came to the surface of the log.

'Oh look,' said Al. 'A cockroach on that log coming out because it's burning.'

'Not, a cockroach in my house!' exclaimed June from the kitchen.

'It's in the fire June, no need to worry,' said Al quietly but with a hint of annoyance.

June belatedly sat to have her tea with the others and asked a few questions of Alice. *A few short questions for starters, just to size me up. She can have my age, rank and serial number but that's all thought Alice rebelliously. She won't get anything too personal.* There were a few questions about her father and mother and family in general which she answered politely. Her family were not famous in any way she knew of but they were kind and worked hard although not in any high paying executive positions. Her dad owned a small banana farm in Queensland and her mother worked in a childcare centre part time in the small town of Maroubra. *Do I have any siblings?* She answered June who was chief inquisitor. 'Yes, I have a brother at the Uni of Queensland and he is studying law/commerce.'

Is it my imagination or is June much more attentive since I mentioned my brother's study? 'Oh – Shelby was studying at the Uni of Queensland wasn't she Geoffrey? Yes, Shelby was a lovely girl, but she and Geoff had a bit of a quarrel and things didn't quite work out so she went up to Queensland...'

Alice's toes curled at this obvious name-dropping June was doing – of Geoff's old girlfriend.

Geoff answered matter-of-factly 'Yeah mum. Shelby's married now too, remember?' He was annoyed that his mum would bring up Shelby in front of Alice. He would hate for Alice to think that Shelby and he were anything more than ancient history. They had grown apart years ago, and were now nothing more than acquaintances on Facebook. June was embarrassed by Geoff exposing her, and quickly changed the subject – not without another little comment thrown in.

'Shelby was a great student – it's good that she pursued her ambitions. Well, I wanted to study nursing, and I did – I was a nurse for a few years...And then I met Al,' said June a little flatly. 'But! Little Geoffrey came along and what better life could I have than to live in the bush with my stand-up comedian husband!' she laughed but Alice noticed that the others didn't. How could she do that to Alpaca? He seemed such a dear man. Not so deep down Alice was kindling hostility towards June. Not only a homemaker extraordinaire but also a home wrecker, a curious combination. Alice asked Geoff to lead her to the toilet, which was just outside in an attached veranda. Once outside the main part of the house she wrenched her arm out of his and snorted like a horse. Geoff was taken by surprise and started back from her. She said an angry whisper: 'You didn't tell me that your mother was so, so well… so. Well anyway she just is really intrusive and obviously she approves of your ex, and even my brother but you're not going out with either of them. Even if something more was to happen between us, I am *not* what she wants for you.'

'Now, now, Alice, you're getting a bit worked up over nothing. Mum is an interrogator but I don't think she means to hurt anyone.'

'I'm feeling pretty inferior at the moment you know, also darned (no I won't upset you by saying the other word although it sounds just the same) angry! She obviously brought up your ex – Shelby – so that I was sure to know about her. And then there's all the bustling around in the kitchen – I know she would like me to offer to help, but how can I when I can't see?'

'Settle down Alice' said Geoff comfortingly (which was something she loved about him – the way he calmed her down). 'Just let it slide, Dad does.'

'I don't think you are very perceptive. I'm blind and even I can tell that she humiliated him – mocking his attempts at comedy.'

'N...No, I... that's not true.' stammered Geoff seeing a side of Alice he had not suspected. It reminded him of a film where some foolish tourist had gotten out of a jeep to take pictures of a group of feeding lions. The best thing to do is not disturb her any more. *She'll go off like a firecracker. Get back in the jeep Geoff.* He had to smile when he saw how impassioned she had become, standing up for his funny stand-up comedian Dad – funny being the debatable word.

'Do you think I'm a freak? I'm blind Geoff, blind, and before I join the circus, I would like you to tell your parents that I am not a strapping hearty country lass. I finished my final year of high school but never went on to do anything good at all! So not only am I blind but I am a blind ignoramus.'

Geoff laughed. He couldn't help himself. She actually said some very amusing things when she was cranky.

'I just wanted them to realise what a nice person you are.'

'Nice person! I'm sorry you got that impression. What 'nice', nice, for a blind girl?

Geoff, if you knew she wouldn't be happy, and be downright passive aggressive, why bring me here? I can feel the vibes of disapproval you know. You know, it's not her fault. She has raised you to have every success in life...as I said – the possibility of a blind girl friend is just not something they can handle.' Every time she mentioned her as his girlfriend, even as a remote possibility, made his heart skip a beat. Despite himself, he smiled at her.

Alice stood mule like with arms folded and jaw set. 'I don't think I want to come in when I am far from welcome, not-good-enough, not accomplished enough!' grumped Alice.

'You are far too touchy. Your perception is far from realistic. Of course, mum will size you up – but I am here to protect you, so don't forget that. You'll get used to them. Leave mum to me to defuse. She's quite a surprise to tread on.'

'And nasty to get off your shoe!' exclaimed Alice expelling a gut felt laugh. She now began to see the lighter side.

'Geoff put an arm around Alice and said, 'It's cold out here. You have to come in.'

She stiffened up and went to pull away.

Alice glared at him and said 'OK, I'm coming in due course.'

'What does in due course mean?' asked Geoff.

'When I'm ready!' she snapped.

Geoff dashed inside letting the old screen door bang. It always banged because it had never been fixed. That wasn't quite true. It had been fixed many a time but even though the men were clever at farming and could fix quite complex machinery they never seemed to manage the kitchen screen door. Geoff returned with an old rug and tenderly wrapped it around her shoulders.

He is really sweet so sweet. Why am I hurting him like this? I have to stop. Bringing me out a rug. Anything to avoid an all-in brawl I suppose, but how caring. He's not the average guy. I don't think I would put up with myself as much as he is putting up with me. I could be imagining the whole scenario with his mum. How can I be sure what she is thinking? I may be being ridiculous. Yep, I'll just let it go – she breathed out through her nose and felt herself relax. She was ready to face them again.

Five minutes later he returned and led her back into the warm room where both parents sat. June and Al were kind, and June took her hands and rubbed them to warm them up. Al put another log on the fire and got out the 'Land' newspaper and commenced to read it. He didn't know what to talk about and would leave it up to June and Geoff to get the ball rolling. He wasn't much of a talker.

Alice would have gladly told them that she was the problem. She was into self-blame at that moment.

'I am sorry I'm blind.' she told them. To her there seemed to be no great drama but then she couldn't see the looks of pity, fear and disappointment that crossed their faces as they sat saying nothing.

'Don't you worry dear.' said June sympathetically. 'You don't have to feel awkward around us, does she?'

Al still held his paper as a kind of escape route should the conversation get too difficult.

'Of course not.' he replied.

'Out here everyone helps everyone else and that's the way we get by.' said June. 'Sometimes a little too much help,' said Al quietly.

'What do you mean by that?' said June shooting her husband the look of death. 'Helping can lead to interfering,' said Al suddenly reading something very interesting in his paper.

'Alice suppressed a giggle, started to snort. She covered her mouth and used a camouflaging cough.

'You see, you've probably caught a chill now.' admonished June in a traditionally motherly way.

'I think a crumb went down the wrong way.' said Alice tapping her throat.

The rest of the evening went by cordially and Alice was still annoyed with June, but (as she said to Geoff later on) it really was not her problem and although Geoff's mother had only been kind to her, she sensed her disappointment. She was not what June had wanted for her son in the way of a girlfriend. *Damn this blindness!* Alice silently fumed. *There Geoff I've said the 'd' word!*

All of this self-deprecation made her started disliking innocent people who only meant well.

'We had to cull some cattle this year,' said Geoff, trying to keep the conversation going.

'Why' asked Alice, 'what was wrong with them?'

Al, Geoff's father spoke. 'Yes, ah, well, things like growths, being too long in the body, bad feet, bad eyes.' Geoff's father looked as though he'd swallowed a spider. He was embarrassed.

'Oh, bad eyes. Mmm, like me,' said Alice sensing the ridiculousness of the situation. 'It's quite OK. Mr Parker, er Al… Paca.' She gave a little giggle. She knew he could kick himself after this faux pas.

'Just call me Al,' said Al. I'm afraid my sense of humour is not always appreciated and rightly so! He grasped her hand and gave it a little squeeze.

'No!' exclaimed Alice 'I think that the Alpaca thing is really clever and funny and I prefer it to Mr Parker if you don't mind. Al smiled in a relieved way and pulled at the collar on his flannelette shirt. He had gone quite a shade of red from his neck to his head after the comment about the bad eyes in cattle. June was curt and said: 'Well Alice, I'll show you around and give you your towel. If you need anything in the night just tap on the wall and I can help.'

Alice felt her cheeks burn. Tapping on the wall was a stunt she would have expected to do as a small child needing adult toilet intervention.

She smiled and nodded, 'Thank you June I'll make sure I give it a good rap but I hope I don't knock any painting down! She realized that this joke was a sinker and a stinker.

June said nothing.

'Gee the fire gets strong, doesn't it?' said Alice.

'Only when you get too close,' said June clicking away with her knitting needles. And a slight sniff.

It looks as if this is the end of the evening. I reckon she would like to cull me from the herd. For a

moment she imagined what it would be like to be June's daughter-in-law and shuddered. She was a model of sheer perfection. She was daunting. *But...she did warm my hand. She is kind. I'm just mean, bitter. I must be better somehow. Lord, please make me nice. I so want to be a nicer person. One day I want to be with you in that glorious place and I don't want the guilt anymore...of having hurt people and made their lives unhappy...* 'Goodnight' Alice said to June and Al as Geoff led her to her room. Outside the room she felt more relaxed. 'Are they around?' she asked Geoff.

'They're in the lounge room.' he answered.

'Goodnight, Geoff and sweet dreams and I'm sorry for my tantrum earlier on. Thank you for taking me here. I can't remember when I last heard kookaburras calling across a valley. It's glorious.' She stood on her tiptoes and gave him a little peck on the cheek. She went into her room and closed the door leaving Geoff wondrously touching the place on his face where she had kissed him. *She's quite complex and I think I will need a degree in psychology to understand her basic emotional requirements.*

He shook his head and smiled. There was hope with this girl, there was definitely hope.

Eight

Before she slept Alice lay in bed thinking. Not too long, just long enough to decide it would be better to be a toleration rather than an irritation to Geoff and his parents. She resolved to be a cheerful helpful guest in their home but not to let her guard down. How would she manage that! It was a paradox. On the one hand she would offer her help, and on the other hand she was keen to be a little aloof. She wanted to keep part of herself (the main part) to herself so that she could monitor what she gave out. No home truths or things said in confidence.

She didn't was to expose herself to a savaging from the bull shark June. Alice gasped at her nasty thoughts and suppressed smile. *I can hardly believe that only a day a go I was in the middle of an oily smoggy city full of train noises and petrol fumes. I can also hardly believe I'm being so uncharitable towards Geoff's mother. Comparing her to a bull shark! It may be partly true but certainly they never swim this far up river.*

She was really starting to relax with a few more Vesuvius like little giggles that made her whole body vibrant with delicious humour. It was lovely here and the fragrance in the air of walnut tree was lulling her to sleep as well as stirring her sense of adventure and love of the bush. Over the valley a flock of white cockatoos shrieked their way through the darkening evening sky and later came the mournful clack, clack, clack of the plovers. The air was cold but full of rich eucalypt fragrance and then there was the unmistakable aroma of sweet grasses and cattle. Alice breathed in deeply and smiled.

The very purity of the air had worn her out and she slept soundly and peacefully.

Morning came with the sweet bewitching music of tiny wrens outside her window. Alice smiled and hopped out of bed. She dressed in a nice warm tracksuit but couldn't find her Ug boots. Geoff knocked at the door which Alice opened smiling pleasantly at him. She really felt pleasant, felt like being a pleasant person today and Geoff was responsible. He noticed how the drawn look she often had about her had gone with the first song of the birds.

'You look great Alice,' he said as he took her arm.

'Wait! Don't you think I've forgotten something? My feet are completely nude. Could you please help me find my Ug boots? Much as I love old wood floors, they are icy on an Autumn morning.

'Sure,' said Geoff, 'I'll find them. No worries. They must be around somewhere or maybe you left them in Melbourne.'

'No! Definitely not! Leave my precious Uggies at home? Not likely!'

'Here they are!' said Geoff triumphantly.

'Where were they?' asked Alice.

'Where you always put them, I'd imagine, under the bed'

'They must have gotten just out of my reach. I don't normally put them under the bed because I'm afraid that mice will nest in them. I usually put them at the on the bed but on top of the bed. You see I have quite a fear of mice.' 'That's why you keep that fearsome cat no doubt.'

'Well, yes we do have a kind of symbiotic relationship.'

'Not really Alice. You care for him and feed him but what does he do for you?'

'Look, he's warm and alive on my bed in Melbourne when I am alone, OK?!

She was on edge again and wanted to start the day on a good note so she squeezed his arm. Geoff smiled fondly at her soft face as they walked to the kitchen.

'You like my ball-y tracksuit? Actually, this is my new lint-free one for special occasions such as random holidays on an Alpaca Farm.'

'Alice, do you never give up?' said Geoff shaking his head and smiling. Sometimes she was too much and he felt like giving her a friendly throttling. They went into the kitchen and sat at the table which was a Laminex with a lattice printed pattern on it. Alice felt the metal rim that went right around it and a misty look came upon her. She remembered that kind of table from long ago at her grandparent's home. Geoff noticed her sad face and passed her the blackberry jam. Nothing could withstand (not even depression) the power of that blackberry jam! Alice munched into her toast and a look of rapture replaced the melancholy. 'Delicious!' was all she could say as she savoured the tart–sweet condiment.

'Eggs and bacon dear?' inquired June kindly and then 'Did you have a nice sleep?' 'It was fine until those wrens started their racket. Oh, yes thank you I haven't had eggs and bacon for ages. That would be absolutely, lovely!'

'I wouldn't call the wrens sound a noise. It's a song. It's music!' said June in a slightly offended tone. Alice tried to say that it was only a joke and that she absolutely treasured the sound of the wrens when June continued talking.

'Well, my dear, while you're here you are going to have a real holiday. And that means plenty of wren song and good food!'

Geoff and his dad smiled at each other and then Al went back to his newspaper. They knew what 'good food' meant.

By the end of the week Alice was to find out what the men's little snigger meant. Before Al and Geoff drove the cattle to safe ground, Geoff hailed Alice at the back gate of the house. She had wanted to pat the horses. The men both rode up and Alice whispered to the horses 'I just want to pat your velvety noses.' Geoff leaned forward and held her hand guiding it to stroke his own nose. 'Velvety enough for you Alice?'

'Not quite the same' she laughed finding his little joke particularly hilarious. Geoff had not heard her really belly laugh like this before and he was very pleased with himself. Al's eyes sparkled too. His son did have a good sense of humour. *Just like his old man!*

'Well, we'll see you at morning tea. In a weeks' time we'll have to shoe horn you into the four-wheel drive.'

'What do you mean? Am I getting fat?'

'You'll find out!' laughed Geoff.

'What *is* this private joke? It's all about food isn't it!'

'Gotta go! See you later, said Geoff squeezing her hand.

Al smiled at the tender exchange of his boy with Alice then turned his horse in the direction of the cattle which couldn't believe their luck being driven upwards to dense lush grass normally not their fare. With the crisis of the rising flood waters, they got to have this special benefit – all of this ungrazed grass made up for the inconvenience of trudging uphill like vast cruising islands in a sea of green. They made quite a bit of noise and some of the younger six-month-olds leapt and bawled in delight, capering around with bursts of explosive energy. Geoff smiled as he watched them and knew that in another six months they would be lounging around chewing their cuds more asleep than awake only using minimal energy to flick flies off with their tails. Alice helped June with the wiping up and did her best to help. Together they fed the chooks grain. Alice really loved this, and said to June.

'It must be lovely to come out here every day...'

'Twice a day!' interrupted June.

'Twice a day then,' laughed Alice. Oh, I could come out here and feed them three times a day or four...'

'Now, now!' said June with something very like a laugh. 'They might be listening and start to expect it.'

'They don't bite do they?' asked Alice tentatively.

'Oh no dear, laughed June. 'Never in a million years would they!'

They took their gumboots off and put them just outside of the verandah. Alice had to wear a pair of Geoff's boots because he naturally had not reminded her to bring a pair. In any case she didn't own any. Being so big they were easy to get off. The 'girls' had time together till morning tea. They awaited the men and June had cooked up a storm as usual.

Alice admired her stamina.

'June, you are an astounding cook. I am quite put to shame.'

'Well dear, you live alone only used to cooking one portion but I on the other hand have to cook for four huge hollow legs.'

'What do you mean?' asked Alice.

'Oh, it's just an expression, hollow legs meaning insatiable appetite. That's what we mean by it out here in the bush.

'Shouldn't that be six hollow legs, counting yourself?'

'Oh dear, I really don't care if I eat at all, just as long as the men have their food.'

'Am I the eighth pair of hollow legs?'

'Well dear,' said June with a tired voice, 'You don't eat as much as I would like. You are only a tiny thing.'

'Thanks June.' smiled Alice.

'Don't take that a s a compliment! You need a bit of extra fat on your bones, especially in the cold weather, to keep you warm.'

To Alice it seemed that they had just cleaned up after breakfast and that now they were preparing more food. Suddenly it was morning tea. The men were back and were eating more. June's glazed fruit cake was quite a work of art and full of finely honed cooking skills. It was decorated with almonds and glacé cherries. Alice wished she could see it. At least she could smell and taste it. June described it very well to her. She decided that if Alice once had sight, she would be able to grasp some kind vision from her memory. 'Thank-you June! Although it sounds pretty, I'm really keen to eat it now because it smells so wonderful! You see my sense of smell is my keenest sense.' 'Oh no!' exclaimed Geoff. 'Don't come near me. I'm sure I stink.'

'Ooh pooh!' said Alice waving her hand in front of her nose and grimacing in mock disgust.

June sniffed 'Now you two just behave yourselves and eat up.'

All was now silent and the silliness had been diffused by June the trouble-shooter. It was quiet although Alice gave a little giggle when she heard the 'splosh' of a fairly large piece of cake falling into her tea. Geoff, (who was always watching her) noticed this and smiled, barely able to restrain a snigger with a mouthful of cake, potentially a war zone. June was not impressed and was secretly happy when her son had a bit of a cough and choke. Unfortunately, she would be the one to sweep up the crumbs.

Al was engrossed in the paper. *Actually,* thought Alice, *He's hiding in the paper.* She could hear the rustling. He was reading it and commented: 'If only this fellow was a relative.'

'Who dear?' asked the curious June.

'Packer, the young one.'

'Why there's a whole 'r' missing from his name!' said June and she was right. 'Well, it's sort of close,' laughed Geoff. There was a blending of the boys and the girls club while they were talking about Al Parker's unrelated relation.

'I think you would at least come up with an 'r' before you could claim to be related Dad. Do you think you could run a media empire?' asked Geoff sagely.

'I tell you what, for what he gets to do it I'd have a darn good try!'

June who had been listening carefully to the conversation decided that it was just so much nonsense and intervened:

'Enough you men! Keep your minds on the job. Do you want some more cake, Al?

Geoff?'

'I've had plenty mum.' said Geoff.

'Me too.' growled Al. 'Alice?' offered June.

'No thanks June, I'm quite full. It was really scrumptious.'

'Now, now, I'm not going to let you get away with only one piece. You need to cover your bones; I know you've heard me say it before. Here, have another slice. It'll do you good.'

'B, but...'

'No more buts, just eat!'

What a tyrant! Alice did however take another bit, and eavesdropped on the boy's conversation.

Alice wanted to be in the boy's club. It was so much more interesting.

Geoff and Al sipped their tea and talked about the impending flooding of the lower paddocks.

'You know it could even snow the way it's been,' said Al gravely.

'Will there be enough to make a snow man?' asked Alice eagerly.

Both men looked at each other with disbelief.

'Your blond roots are coming through Alice,' said Geoff.

'What is wrong with a snowman?' she asked.

'It's not Mt Hotham love,' said Al kindly, which Alice thought sounded condescending but then she abandoned that idea because Al Paca had only ever been sweet to her and she doubted if he was indeed capable of being condescending.

'I know it's not a ski resort.' continued Alice with an 'of course I realize that!' kind of laugh, then said: 'I could still make a snowman, couldn't I?'

Geoff nodded to her. 'Yes – I promise that if it snows enough, that's what we'll do.' Al sighed, 'It would be a change. 'I haven't even thought about snow men in all these years. You see love, it doesn't often snow this low down and it's usually gone soon after it falls.'

'Why?' asked Alice.

'Melts,' said Al.

'Come on eat up,' said June, 'I made a jam roll this morning and it's just sitting there!'

June (secretly annoyed that the two 'boys' didn't find

her cakes as entertaining as Alice) encouraged Alice to eat. Subconsciously, June thought they only liked her for her food. *I wouldn't mind making a snowman but I suppose I'm too old now. I've missed the boat. I bet they don't even think I would like to make a snow man. It's so sad. And here is this young thing excited about a snowman and now they are too.*

'Jam roll anyone?' she asked again but the subject had changed back to cakes which is what she wanted anyway.

'Come on Alice dear, it wouldn't hurt you to fatten up a bit.'

Alice bit her lip and took a piece. *'Yep, this is what it is, a piece of sponge rolled up with jam in the middle, delicious! At this rate I'll double my weight every week like a duckling. All this good tucker!*

'Come on Geoff,' urged Al. 'Let's get those fences fixed and the gate near the poplars.

I'm sick of the C.O.D. gates, heartily sick of them!'

'C.O.D. gate?' asked Alice, 'What are they?'

'Carry or drag.' laughed Al.

Alice smiled and gave a little snort which Geoff found quite entrancing.

She spent the morning reading her Braille novel out in the sitting room. She was facing the window, and though she couldn't see it, she could smell and hear the wood fire crackling softly. The immense backdrop of silence that was being in the bush. Only the long lonely calls of currawongs and kookaburras would occasionally enter her silence, also, June's rattling of pots and pans in the kitchen intermittently interrupted her. She felt so relieved to be in another place – yet still not quite 100% relaxed due to June's constant fussing about food. Little did she know that June was resenting her in the kitchen, wishing that Alice would come and help.

Meanwhile, Geoff and his dad went to work fixing a few fences and came back at about twelve for some lunch which was roast leg of lamb and baked vegetables, mint sauce and gravy. Alice could feel her stomach lining digesting itself in anticipation. Her stomach growled like a rampaging bear but the weather report on the radio masked the sound. *It's amazing how used to all this food one gets.*

It was really tasty and satisfying but Alice could almost feel the new layer of fat taking its place around her belly.

Bread and butter pudding with cream and raspberries was the finale of the meal. *As if two kinds of cakes wouldn't be enough, she has to make a pudding! What a woman!* Alice was glad she was wearing a stretchy banded tracksuit rather than jeans. If she had jeans on, she would have had to undo the belt several notches. She didn't say so but she now understood the shoe horn joke. She had suspected it anyway right from the start. She certainly couldn't say anything in front of June! It was alright for the men to eat so much because they worked it off. June prattled on about making Al some more shirts. Alice couldn't believe her ears. Making shirts out of flannelette material when she could buy them cheaper at any discount clothing store already made?! June definitely needed a trip to town. No not to town which was a modest place with a supermarket, a chemist and a rural supply store. No, she needed to go to a mall where pretty things dangled at eye level everywhere. She would benefit from the sheer frippery of it, a striking comparison to the code of eating and frugality.

She would never convince June that cheaper shirts could be bought ready so she 'ahhuh' and 'a-hummed' like a doctor examining a patient but not actually wanting an encounter. She just couldn't get into a debate about a flannelette shirt.

Across the laden lunch table, Geoff said: 'I'll take you riding tomorrow Alice, along the top of the property. It's really beautiful, you know and we might even see...'

'Geoff!' June's sharp voice filled the room. She felt that talking about 'seeing' to a blind girl was gauche, utterly.

'S, sorry,' said Geoff looking down and like a whipped pup then continued eating.

Alice couldn't see his face but her heart went out to Geoff because he of all people considered her feelings the most.

'It's alright,' said Alice, 'just pretend I'm like the rest of you.' She realized her comment sounded even worse than she intended. *Yes, she thought bitterly I'm not the same though am I, I'm disabled. I'm different, a second-class citizen and certainly not someone a strapping country boy should be interested in.* She kept it to herself obviously and anyway what else could she do.

Then annoyingly she heard herself saying 'Really, I'm pretty thick-skinned June.' She could shrug off Geoff's comment easily but found the overreaction of his mother quite a different matter.

She normally didn't think of herself as blind but the truth of the matter was that she was.

June and Al looked at each other tight-lipped.

'Do you think bicarb of soda has to go in scones?' asked Alice breezily (Having once read about it). Sometimes I think it's better to use plain flour and add bicarb rather than trust out of date self-raising flour. What do you think June?

Before she could answer Alice thought: *Well frankly June, I don't – can't – won't – ever make scones, so do I really know or care how they are made!*

'I suppose I'm somewhat of an expert when it comes to scones.' said June modestly. 'And I think experts like your-self should be the only ones to make them.' said Alice decisively.

June smiled 'Why thank you Alice! What a compliment!'

I'm full of them thought Alice.

Geoff looked on amused. He knew Alice was smart, but this cunning was the stuff of legends to be immortalized at some point in time but he was glad that his mum had missed the joke. Even though his dad had a childish sense of humour it was at least some sense of humour! Poor mum just seemed too keen to be sensible. It occurred to him that she needed a holiday in much the same way that Alice had to have one. She was the censor of the family, and tried to stop anything that she deemed to be wrong whether it was talking about seeing around a blind person, or slipping the odd swear word. It was not as though he meant to swear, just that at sometimes it was a real release and the trick was to do it when she wasn't around. Geoff remembered clearly when he was about ten and a wasp was hovering around him in the garden. All he could manage to do was say SHIT very loudly for which he was sent to his room for the afternoon.

Alice's sudden interest in scone making was ingenious even though fake. She had cleverly gotten his mother off the tunnel vision of June's – the subject of Alice's disability.

Tomorrow they would ride in the bush, just her and him, free from domestic duty. Alice resented the god-like treatment that men received in this household. *Men are useful, I suppose* she thought.

Geoff asked Alice what kind of sandwiches he should make, and they both settled on egg, gherkin and cream cheese, so that they could avoid obligatory lunch at the house.

Geoff smiled at the thought of their uninterrupted day together.

'What's this?!' exclaimed June observing the sandwiches in the fridge.

'Just some food for our picnic tomorrow, 'said Geoff, as casually as he could manage.

'Dear, I would have made you some nice ones!' she said mournfully.

'It's OK mummy, they are yummy.' laughed Geoff giving June a cuddle causing her to giggle with joy.

'Well, I hope you used the fresh bread I made.'

'Yes, I certainly did. To be sure to be sure.'

Alice, who had been observing the whole scenario could no

longer hold herself back and contributed to the conversation.

'How couldn't the sandwiches not be good, made with your lovely homemade bread!' 'Yes, I suppose you're right.' agreed June who then went off pottering around polishing the kitchen sink.

Geoff leant over to Alice as surreptitiously as he could and whispered: 'I think I am madly smitten with you, for your sheer cunning!'

'I aim to please.' said Alice smugly. 'By the way I'm going to check on Tabby again, if you care to join me. I don't think he likes you though, so don't expect him to rub around your legs. Do you think I can let him out of the washhouse soon? He must be getting bored in there....'

'Or maybe he's become an exterminator, terminating the lives of hapless mice.' They walked out through the verandah, towards the washhouse. It was a long decommissioned wooden building, suitable for Tabby to live. It was dusty, but warm and fairly neat.

'Well Geoff, at least he's being useful out here, like you men.'

'Yes, I suppose I *am* useful.' he smiled.

'Not like me.' Alice said. 'I'm just no good at all. I've made myself useless and it's all my own doing.'

'Oh Alice, just stop it. Tabby is useful and so are you. I saw you feeding the chooks. They seemed pleased about that and I saw you scraping the mud off my boots (and so you should since you got them dirty!) which are useful things to do.' 'Of course, you encourage me. How can I be useful though, when I am so sight challenged? I just sat around reading for most of the day yesterday. I mean, it was peaceful and all, but you know I'd like to be doing something useful. There's no way I can help your mum in the kitchen for example. I wouldn't know where to start – so I don't even try.'

'Don't worry Alice you have more than enough deviousness to get by anywhere.' 'You think I'm cunning! I'm just trying to survive in the rarefied atmosphere of your mum's home – not that I'm criticising her!'

'Come on tiger, let's check the other little tiger – your cat.' With that he took her arm and they went to check the cat. Alice's stomach disappeared two foot below her feet when he took her arm. *What is wrong with me!? she reminded herself – We're just friends. He is just a kind man. And how could I betray Stephen by such feelings? Alice, get a grip!*

As they approached the wash house and he could hear him meowing.

'He loves me!' exclaimed Alice with joy.

So do I. Thought Geoff earnestly, but he tried to hide his feelings. *I'll do what Dad told me to do when we were watching birds. Don't make a noise that will frighten them. Just let them go about doing what they do and keep your distance. They'll get used to you and sooner or later they will take food from out of your hands. Remember, don't go too fast. It might take weeks, as long as it takes, as long as it takes.*

Nine

The air was fresh and bitter the next morning, typical Autumn, as Alice and Geoff went to the yard. Geoff's favourite trees were there as always, and hopefully would be for another hundred years. How he wished Alice could see them. The claret ash in rich burgundy leaf contrasted with the bright yellow golden ash beside it. Soon the soft green grass would be coated with a rich carpet of red and yellow fallen leaves. Geoff enticed the horses over with a bucket of oats (they needed enticing, as they had worked really hard the day before and were a little jaded and stiff), but the smell of oats made them forget their previous exploitation, while they ate he saddled them up. 'That's enough Nobby!' said Geoff wrenching the horse's chomping mouth out of the bucket. Bits of food: oats, bran, lucerne chaff, oaten chaff, molatin and livermol were being dropped in colourful sprinkles everywhere as the horses gobbled as much food as they could.

'It's an appetizer! You'll be sick if you eat too much before exercise. I know it's delicious but you two can have the rest later, something to look forward to.'

Geoff smiled as he said this, and thought just how much these horses were like people to him, in much the same way Tabby was to Alice. 'Stop, stop you crazy horses! You'll be totally bloated!'

'I know the feeling,' laughed Alice dryly.

'Yes, mum does load up the plates,' Geoff chuckled. 'But no one's forcing you to eat it, are they?!'

'Yes, I agree, the food is unbeatable and it's not torture at the time, but when I try to squeeze into clothes and have gone up a size it's not fun, I assure you! And say no to your mother? You must be crazy! I reckon you could make a trip to the North Pole and back fuelled on one of her roast dinners and really, seriously have you ever tried to say no to your mum when she badgers you to tuck in?'

'To cover your bones!' laughed Geoff.

'Or be incapacitated and not able to walk to the end of the yard!'

'You know what they say 'feed the man meat.'

'Or woman!' spluttered Alice.'

'You just told me you got too much roast beef.'

'It's the principle.' Alice smiled but was giggling inside.

'Whether I eat it or not is not the issue!'

Geoff helped her up onto the horse and fastened a lead rein to it. They rode up through the bush until the house was far below. The sound of the leaf litter under hoof, and the pungent smells emanating from it drew Alice back to the world she had once loved.

Though she didn't show it, she was having a spiritual experience. *You must still be God. You're still here in this world. I can feel you. I can smell you. I know you're here. Please forgive me*

for doubting you, yes, I do love you still and I am going try to trust
you again.

Geoff smiled as he looked at Alice. She was so pretty. He just wanted to lean over and kiss her, but decided it might spoil everything. At the worst she may slash him with her cat paws full of claws!

The 'carry or drag' gates were hellish. Alice had to hold onto Nobby's reins while Geoff struggled with them.

'Is that a swear word I hear?' asked Alice loudly perched atop Goldy, a chestnut mare, with a cheeky smile.

'You have a great imagination.' Geoff puffed and hopped back onto his horse again.

'I thought you and your dad fixed all of the gates?'

'There are a lot of gates.' was all he replied.

He too was awake to the beauty of the bush, and who had made it all. Geoff wasn't a great church-goer, but did love God and wished he could encourage Alice that they were part of a bigger beautiful picture. It was easy to believe here. Anyway, she seemed to be right at home here.

Now they went downward into a dank, eucalyptus smelling gully.

'Whoops!' she laughed as Goldy's hind quarters sank down and her hind feet tried to grip as she slipped down the muddy slope. The reins slipped out of Alice's hands as the horse pitched and Geoff scooped them up and gave them back to her.

'Why thank you Rhett.' Alice said in a southern belle accent that would have made Scarlett O'Hara proud.

'No problem little lady,' answered Geoff, imitating Rhett Butler quite well.

In the shadows, Goldy, whose chestnut coat normally shone like burnished copper, had gone a shade of dark chocolate, saturated with sweat. At the bottom of the gulley, Geoff and Alice got off the horses to give them a rest. They tied the horses nearby, and meanwhile Geoff and Alice found a comfortable seat on a log next to a stream. The babbling water blended with the twittering wrens and for a long time the two sat, not talking but simply absorbing the essence of the bush. Every so often a loud bird (usually a cockatoo) would disturb the silence, an assault for the ears, and yet it belonged. From someplace came the thrillingly exquisite almost hissing call of the golden whistler. It made one wish to stay forever, and that forever was as real a place as the here and now. The twittering of the blue wrens was in her soul. She decided she would always remember this no matter how dark her days in Melbourne may get.

Geoff gazed at Alice, wishing she could love him, willing her to in his mind. Yet, he didn't want to frighten her away. Instead, he enjoyed the closeness of sitting next to her on the log.

'I've been hankering for those sandwiches we made.' he said.

Snapping out of her reverie, Alice said 'Ooh yes, me too.'

So, they munched quietly in the clearing, enjoying the supreme peace of the bush bird symphony.

Alice didn't talk much on the way back and Geoff found that

every conversation he attempted to start up was cut rather short. She seemed preoccupied, in another world. To venture here could be dangerous because when she was like this, she was a bit like a cornered animal, likely to strike out indiscriminately. Biting as it were, the very hand that fed her, fed her love and adoration and every good thing he could think off. As the horse's rhythmic footfalls crunched along the bush track, he noticed her stern expression, quite a frown. He decided to try once again to get to the bottom of it, which would help him, possibly, and also help her, possibly.

'Alice?'

'Yes.'

'You know that I'm just a dumb man and don't know much.'

'Yes.'

'Well, if there is anything you want to talk about – anything, please feel free to talk…about it.'

'It?'

'Do you want to?'

'No.' said Alice firmly.

'No what?' asked Geoff.

'No thank you Geoff.'

'Well, that's better.'

Alice shrugged and looked a little defiant which was one of her common expressions when she talked to Geoff but he could see the corner of her mouth turn up and knew he had succeeded in amusing her.

They gave the horses a rub down and released them to roll in the yard. The caked on sweat mixed with dirt was going to be hard to get off later, but Geoff allowed his horses this simple pleasure. They looked dishevelled but happy as they got up and had a big shake. Bits of stuff: leaves dirt, hair filled the air around them. Good to stay away if you were allergic to any of it.

They put the saddles away in the shed and finally got the courage to speak up. He could have circled around the uncomfortable silence saying something vacuous and non-confrontational but he had to know what was going on with her.

'What's the matter Alice? I thought we could spend a bit of time together today and relax. I've got to help Dad a fair bit for the rest of the week. Let's just have fun now while we can.'

'I can't understand why you would want to spend time with me.' she said sadly turning away.

'What do you mean? You are very entertaining in your caustic little way you know? Yes, surprise, surprise! I really *love* being with you and I thought you liked being out here.

Didn't you like it, the bush I mean, the ride? What did I do wrong?'

Alice turned to face him and this time Geoff could see tears welling up in her lovely clear blue eyes.

'Can't you see that I'll never be any good for you? I'll always be a nuisance, a shadow following you around. Your parents are kind, but I know what they really want for you, and it's not me. If I was a cow (and I guess I am in a way) you would cull me, kill me because I am faulty, not productive.'

'Dad's comment was a mistake he wishes like heck he could retract! He loves you, you know and...'

'Let me finish!' said Alice. 'I think you will just have to let me go because I can't even stand myself and you are a really nice person.'

'I'm *Nice!*' exclaimed Geoff in horror 'I would rather you called me a rat, because even rats have personality. You will never know how 'nice' hurts. You might as well say I am a nothing. If you want me to be bad, I can be. I can be whatever you want.'

With that she turned, and when Geoff laid a hand on her arm, she shooed him away. Reluctantly she took his arm and with a disdainful sniff wiped her eyes and went with him back to the house.

Geoff thought: *This girl is harder to tame than any pig-headed horse. So hard to know, and yet I want to know her so much.*

Once inside the warm house in the living room with the fire radiating volumes of heat, Alice became the perfect sociable guest asking all the right questions of June such as: how are the shirts going? how did the sponge rise? etc. Geoff was observing her every move. *Maybe that's what she doesn't like about me, that I'm following her around all the time like a faithful kelpie? Even faithful kelpies become annoying when they jump up on you with muddy feet and lick you in the face after eating a cow pat. I haven't actually licked her face with cow pat tongue.* He smiled at the thought of her reaction if he told her what he was thinking. *I'm not very good at putting on an act. Maybe*

I should be more aloof. She might like that, but when I see her unhappy my gut instinct is to cuddle her and wipe her tears away. She's so darned attractive. I can barely keep my hands off her but I will. When I went to the zoo a tiny mouse deer came up to me. Only the size of a rabbit really. I put my hand out to it and it was coming up to me but I got scared it might bite me so I pulled back. Alice reminds me of that mouse deer and I'm just going to have to hold off being affectionate with her at least for the time being.

The week went by in a fairly boring way for Alice. She read braille books, romance novellas mainly, but they made her cry. The heroine always ended up with the man of her dreams and the man of *her* dreams was still Stephen. The day she and Geoff went riding she nearly told him about her ill-fated loved affair. June while ironing kept making comments like:

'I've never read a romance novel. They are so trivial and unrealistic. Where are you ever going to find someone as wishy washy as those heroes? A man who is full of romantic talk isn't a real man as far as I'm concerned. I've never had flowers from Al and I would suspect something if he did give them to me.'

'I'll remember that.' muttered Alice under her breath.

'Pardon dear?'

'Oh nothing', replied Alice thinking, *anyone would be wishy washy compared to you June.*

'How do you feel about flowers Alice?' asked June still ironing.

'I think they are nice.'

'They are nice in the garden. Although, if cut they die too

quickly.' June was very practical.

'But isn't it the thought that counts? Yes, they do die so quickly but the fact that someone would spend a lot of money knowing that, is quite admirable.'

'Not out here in the bush!' snorted June.

Geoff was taking mental notes jotting up all of this. 'What kind of flowers do you like Alice?' he asked.

'I must say the roses are hard to beat for the smell.'

'I have a whole garden of them, no need to buy any, waste of money.' Said June decisively.

The highlight of her day was when Geoff took Alice for a walk. The smell of the snow gums and tee tree was invigorating and gave her a wild longing in her soul for who knows what? Maybe it was the promise of heaven, that elusive place which gave hints of itself in the world she lived in now. The sound of the creek was as old as time, and she sometimes she wished she could become a stream and be carried away trickling to freedom.

'This is my special paddock,' said Geoff. 'My endurance horses are here. I breed them. Here's Carla's foal. It's four months old.'

Alice touched the tremulous velvety soft nose of the foal and smiled.

Geoff smiled to see her smiling. *She can enjoy herself when she let go of her worries, when she stops trying to analyse every moment of happiness and whether she is worthy of it.*

'Oooh, how beautiful,' she murmured. 'What is his name?'

'Well, it's actually 'Jasper's Pride' after his father – Jasper, he's a well-known stock horse.'

After a pause, Alice said 'I wish I was a foal out here in the bush.' Nothing to do all day but enjoy the most beautiful scenery on God's Green Earth – if I could see.' 'You did once, didn't you, Alice? You never talk about it but you do remember these scenes, don't you?' He wondered how this had happened to her, but didn't ask her, believing she would tell him when and if she felt ready.

'I wasn't a child when I went blind. I remember a lot.'

'What do you remember?' Geoff asked gently.

'This, the bush. But I don't want to talk about it now. It just makes me sad. One day we can talk about it but not now.'

'That's OK Alice. At least you can smell it and feel it and hear it.'

'I know, but not seeing it is so hard for me. I should be...I would...I don't want to be blind. I want to run and kick up my heels and shake my mane.' she smiled 'You're a regular little pony!' laughed Geoff tousling her hair.

'And I might kick!' she added with a toss of her head and flaring nostrils.

'What? Kiss?' asked Geoff.

'KICK!'

Geoff had said enough along that line and decided to be sensible now.

'This coming Saturday is the Mountain Men's endurance ride. I'm taking Smithy here,' said Geoff placing Alice's hand on the

Arab gelding's wrinkled nose. Its lip twisted around to grasp a carrot and not drop it. Alice held Smithy's top lip which moved side to side like the blue tongue lizard she had once saved off a road. She had it by the back of its neck and it was heavy and heaving side to side like a ball of muscle, like this horse upper lip! He won't bite me, will he?'

'Smithy? Not in a million years! He's bomb proof. I can even vault up onto his back from behind and he doesn't stop eating or even lift his head up to take notice. I can sit on him backwards and ride him, mind you only at a walk. It's a real party trick.'

'Why Smithy? Why are you riding him in the race? And how did you name him?'

'Well, there was another Smithy who was a friend of Dad's, an old guy who'd ridden in the light horse brigade at Beersheba in the first World War. He was a real old battler who could tell a yarn. I figured with a name like Smithy this horse would have to be a trier, one to never say die.'

'Old Smithy is tough but gentle like this Smithy. He'll tackle the roughest country but he would never think to tip me off his back, just wouldn't enter his mind. He's a real trier…That's what you're like Alice, a real trier and a real terrier.' he laughed.

'That's a really sweet thing to say Geoff, that I'm a trier but I don't know whether being a terrier is a compliment. I'm afraid I don't cope too well with my excess baggage or even with compliments. Just know that even if I don't look happy about it, I really do love you saying kind things to me. It's a reflex action to reject kindness when it's offered.'

'People don't say nice things about you unless they are true.' said Geoff.

'It's all about guilt and having let others down.'

'You haven't let me down and you *are* a trier even if you haven't killed a rat like a good terrier.'

'What on earth do you mean Geoff, now I'm a ratter? And I'm supposed to be accepting that as a compliment!'

'Rats as big as themselves?'

'Yep, you're getting the picture.'

'But I could never kill a rat.' She sighed in frustration. 'What do you mean?'

'I mean that if you were a terrier, you would. You're brave.'

'I don't recall ever being brave.'

'You are. You stand up for yourself and even when mum drives you crazy you just file it away and let it go.'

'I may file stuff away, but I don't let it go – readily that is'

'You are always sweet to her, and you are gracious enough and clever enough to have your little victories but not in a hurtful way.'

'Yeh, I suppose you're right but you've got to see why I never fight back. It's because she is your mum and I could never hurt you like that.'

'But if you got the chance to be horse, you would kick me?'

'Oh, I'd say anything to stir you, you know that by now.' Alice turned and faced away from him hoping he wouldn't see the tell-tale signs of her affection for him.' She was going back to Melbourne soon and away from this glorious place and away from him. *Probably for the best* she thought. He can get on with finding a wife, a strong sturdy one that makes good scones.

'Terriers are small but brave and they kill rats.' he insisted.

'Yes, Geoff but what about the cats? *They* don't get any special adulation for catching rats, and they have to stay outside but I bet a ratting terrier would get to stay right near the fire and fart it's little heart out!'

'What!?' Alice! I hope I didn't hear what I think I just heard? I am shocked and horrified. No girl would ever say such a thing let a long do such a thing.'

Alice sniggered which turned into helpless laughter until she could barely stand.

Geoff stood watching her with a shake of his head he wondered if this could be the same shy girl, he had met a month ago at Jacquie's party. So fragile, so demure. This was a new side to Alice that he had not suspected, but then again as he thought about the things she had been saying lately it probably wasn't such a surprise. He liked it.

They made their way back slowly from the horse paddocks.

He is still on about that terrier that I am supposed to be. Much as I like him, he is a repetitious creature. Alice thought to herself. *I wish I could tell him about Stephen, how guilty I felt that I wasn't with him that day. Maybe this is the time to tell him? Should he know I abandoned Stephen? How I miss him. I'll never have his children. I think I am letting go of him, after all there's not much I can do about it now. He is in heaven, happy as can be, surrounded by his people, but I still have to go home to my flat. This year I'll do a course of some kind, maybe even try to get into Uni. Who knows what lies ahead? Actually, despite myself, I think things are looking up. Geoff is just like a brother to me…except wanting to kiss me. A little peck is one thing, but a big one is weird. Having him around is nice. He talks to me. I am going to be as nice as I can for the rest of the time I'm here. There's something about Geoff that I want. His positive kind nature. He never wants to fight, although I've given him plenty of opportunity to. He's brotherly but there is something else. I just don't want to think about that! I don't want to burden Geoff with all of my miseries. He wants to help but he is needed here in the bush with his family and I will have to go back – yep back to the big bad polluted, noisy city. That is my fate for the time being, a fair-weather friend to Stephen. Will I tell Geoff? Will I not tell Geoff? To do or not to do, that is the question. He seems to think very highly of me but I'll be gone soon.* She kept everything about Stephen secret. She had let him down, and was bound to let Geoff down as well.

They walked and talked, interesting stuff but not deep and meaningful. Geoff was anticipating the coming endurance race and Alice could sense his excitement. Over the next week they went down to see the mare and her foal a few more times. It was a fair walk but she was getting to know the way and it was a delight to reach the gate and the lovely horses who always seemed so pleased to see them, especially since they always brought a few carrot tops, crusts and cores.

'This is it.' he said.

'What?'

'This is the end of the paddock, and beyond is bush and plenty of it. This is where we ride, along a fire trail right up high to the high plains.'

'You mean that we were up high on the top of the range?'

'Yep, and Goldy nearly took a plunge into the stream with you, remember?'

'She could have tossed me into the icy mountain stream in the middle of Autumn.' Then changing the subject, she asked 'How far back does it go?' she asked.

'As the crow flies it's about eight miles from Bogong – and for your information Goldy was tired but not malicious. I don't keep horses that aren't quiet. And by the way you might do well to copy the horses. They are quiet, and that means as you know that they are gentle. You need a little gentling my girl.' He put his hand gently on her neck and stroked her in the much the same way he might have stroked one of his horses.

'Watch out!' exclaimed Alice, and flinched away from him.

'What's that? Was there a spider?!' exclaimed Geoff with a laugh in his voice.

What did I just say? Oh, my goodness, pull yourself together. Cringed Geoff inwardly.

'I think there might be a pimple on my neck. As a matter of fact, I am sure there is one!' Geoff thought she was hideous but funny, and obviously trying to avoid his overture of affection without embarrassing him. Alice said: 'It a huge one – like Mt Bogong – we were talking about that. Please keep telling me. You were saying – Mt Bogong? It's the highest mountain in Victoria, the second highest in Australia?'

'Go to the top of the class Alice!' Geoff laughed.

'Was I showing off? Yes, don't answer that. It can be a burden being so clever, although I do my best to be humble as you well know.'

'Humble Alice? I always feel I should have an encyclopedia under my arm when I talk to you.'

'An encyclopedia under your arm is not necessary, just deodorant!' with that she spun around quickly and faced Geoff defiantly with a wicked grin. She was flirting with him now.

Geoff couldn't help himself, and clasped her to himself and kissed her.

At once she struggled free and panted in shock.

'I'm sorry.' said Geoff but he knew that she was like the mouse deer he had now frightened into the undergrowth.

'It's alright.' whispered Alice. 'I was being silly and I carry on the teasing a bit much.' 'Alice, I find you exasperating. Do you know how pretty you are and how, how kissable?'

He continued. 'Being around you is like the day at my grandparent's house…'

'Oh no.' giggled Alice not another saga.

'Don't interrupt, it's rude, as I was saying…when we were having a roast dinner…'

'No Geoff! Not about food again!'

'Just listen, it's pretty funny. There was no-one in the room and all the plates were on the table. I saw what I thought was a roast potato and stole it off the plate. It wasn't a potato. It was a parsnip which tasted so bad that I nearly threw it up. Of course, I had to eat it because otherwise I would be caught.'

'Well!' laughed Alice, 'How do you compare me with this little anecdote?'

'You are the delicious potato that turns out to be a parsnip.'

'That's awful! Just because you don't like parsnips doesn't mean that they are bad, just that you jumped in and stole something you shouldn't have!'

'Seriously though you are the most adorable girl in the world and if you jump in my face with that crazy cheeky look, I can't promise that the same won't happen again.' Alice turned and walked stopped and waited. Geoff came up behind her and she took his arm. Now that they had both settled down Geoff looked into the not-so-distant mountain.

'Yep, that's it. She's such a beauty when the snow's on her.' said Geoff gazing in rapture at the mountain. It's Autumn now, you should see it later on.'

'When it has snow. Exactly, I can't see it can I. We can't share that I'm afraid.' she stated plainly. *I'm no good for you. I'm sulky and vindictive just listen to me!* she thought.

'Heck I didn't mean…I'm sorry!' exclaimed Geoff attempting to divert her misery.

'No, no that's fine.' she gazed sadly and gripped his arm as they continued walking.

'You are clever and funny enough to get through your depression and I am here to help you. You know that don't you?' he said.

'I'm despondent.'

'Another big word.' said Geoff knowing full well what she had said.

She continued. 'I can't just be happy for you that you can enjoy all of this.' She swept her arms wide to indicate the vastness of the bush. 'You always seem to be so happy, happy, happy, happy!' she gasped as she drew in breath to keep up the attack. 'I don't want to see you unhappy, really I don't, and your mum and dad deserve more for you than me.'

'Alice if only you knew how I feel about you'

Her heart stopped for a moment. He was actually going to say it – out loud. How he felt for her. All the week he had been sweet, attentive, a bit flirty, but nothing more than a nice friend.

'I would give up all of this to be with you.'

She gazed downward, fearful that he would kiss her again, but wishing he would at the same time.

'I love your sense of humour and your little cranky attacks. I like the way you wage guerrilla warfare on my mum. You're cunning in ways I can only dream of. If it weren't for your bad opinion of yourself, you could be a movie star. You're beautiful!'

'Geoff!' exclaimed Alice with a coy smile. A movie star –

surely not.

'Yep, I kid you not.'

'You know it's not that I want to hurt you. It's just I have secrets that are practically bursting to get out of me. I am not really ready to tell you yet. This week in the bush has been like a romantic novel and you are the protagonist male who if I would love if I could...but, but I can't. I'm sorry.'

'As I was saying Alice. I am unable to be hurt by you. I think of you as a precocious, funny friend and that is enough for me – at the moment.'

'Have you quite finished? I think my ego has overblown with all of that praise, except that being labelled precocious is not really a compliment that I treasure. I'm not used to compliments in general. You could be a politician Geoff if you say your words right. If you play your cards right'.

'Let's go back to the house. In fact, I really think I should be going back to the city. I'm no help with the horses, or in the kitchen with your mum. I'm just stringing you along. I'd be better back in Melbourne typing or weaving baskets. Better to be useless there than useless here. I want to go, please...'

Geoff was quiet for a minute of two and gazed at the lovely Mt Bogong. A small tear slipped from his eye and down his cheek. He wiped it away and was glad she couldn't see it.

'How do I feel about you?' He said mustering up a cheerful voice when all he felt like doing was crying and that was something for him who cried when his dog died and never had since. 'I don't think you're useless I think you are absolutely, ooh just gorgeous, the best thing since sliced bread!'

'Wow!' Alice laughed in spite of herself, 'Some endorsement, However I would prefer to be thought of as a crusty Italian loaf!' she didn't even know that she had hurt Geoff and continued to banter and tease as if she had said nothing of consequence. She had told him she couldn't love him. And that had hurt him, like a blackberry thorn, poisonous and deep.

'Well, you certainly can be crusty!' said Geoff hoping she would suddenly giggle, which she did.

'At least stay till Sunday, after the race? I need you to be here when I get back.' 'OK.' said Alice 'But it goes against the grain. The whole grain actually.' She tried to be amusing for him, but then every so often she would need to tease.

'I'll stay till Sunday.' she said absently and started to walk in the direction of the house. Geoff took her hand and felt it become a tense little claw. It made him feel sick and yet he knew that if he took her in his arms she might react violently, maybe even nip him.

She could be a vicious little vixen.

'Why are you so tense?' he asked gently.

'I'm a *nothing*, didn't you know. How could you ever be happy with me?'

'That's not true!' said Geoff frowning in concern. 'You're definitely something.'

'Oh, you never take me seriously.'

He went to put an arm around her shoulder but Alice sensed his closeness and shrank away.

He was wounded but was sensible enough to realise that she was not angry or repulsed with him, but with herself.

Geoff had a deep belief in God but hadn't shared this with Alice. He wanted to wait till the time was right.

'Alice,' he said 'I love you and God loves you too you know. Jesus knows how you feel and he will make it right. In my eyes and God's eyes you're perfect. Maybe we'll get a miracle. I've been praying you'll get your sight back.'

'Thank you, Geoff,'. Alice felt stunned, this man believed as she did, about God. 'Let's say there's unfinished business between myself and God.' She felt her throat constrict with emotion, always bubbling not too far away.

'Would it help to talk Alice?' asked Geoff. 'I am a good listener – for a bloke – and I wouldn't make you feel bad no matter what story you have to tell. Nothing would make me feel any different about you. Your heart is in good keeping with me.' 'I know Geoff.' she sobbed quietly to herself and tears rolled down her cheeks. She turned away from him.

Geoff tenderly turned her shoulder towards him and wiped her eyes with a freshly ironed hanky.

'Thank goodness for your ironing mother,' she laughed through her tears.

'I'm far too miserable to be around you Geoff. You should meet someone better. I'm afraid I'm one of the back-slidden from God.

I sort of don't trust him.'

'You will again, I'm sure.' said Geoff. 'You just need to be kinder to yourself and while you're at it you could be kinder to me.' he joked. But truer words were never said, and he knew it.

'Of course! I *am* bad to you aren't I! I'm not used to being, well, adored the way you seem to.'

'Yes, I do adore you but I'm still a bloke. All I want to do is make you happy.'

Alice could feel her cheeks heat up. 'Being adored is a new experience for me.' (Which was true, she had not been treated this way even from Stephen.)

'I know you're disappointed with God, but just hang in there and it'll all work out I'm sure it will.' said Geoff as he patted her kindly on the shoulders. She wasn't tensing up this time.

She hadn't told him a thing. *Patience is the name of the game* Geoff told himself *and if that's what it took to know her then that is what he would be patient and gentle. Eventually she will thaw out. Spring is a few long months away. If only the days could be sunny and fragrant with blossom. She would love that. I will wait and wait as long as I have to.*

Ten

The day of the ride had come and Geoff was up before the birds, feeding, watering and generally tending his horses. Alice had Geoff set her alarm clock and she went with him to the yard. Geoff was quiet quieter than usual and Alice kept her silliness and self-hatred to herself, and was a helpful as possible.

Saturday had come quickly but not quickly enough for Alice, as she was hoping to spend some quality time away from Geoff's parents, particularly his mother. She stuck with him and dreaded the time she would be spending in June's kitchen. There was plenty to do, such as getting his gear ready, paying special attention to girths. If they caused bad chaffing on the horse he would be vetted out of the race. If a girth gall formed, it took a couple of weeks to heal. So, Geoff had placed the whole girth in a sheep-skin sleeve which tended to stop the dragging of hair around the chest. Geoff walked around the horses, speaking kind words to them patting them. He was hoping that they didn't pick up his nerves.

'I'm a bit uptight Alice.' said Geoff.

'Yes, you are.'

'What? Am I being cranky?'

'No, but I can tell.'

'How?'

'Being blind I can pick up on nervous movement.'

'Really' Geoff was genuinely fascinated.

'Don't worry, you'll be right.'

'But how do I get rid of this, this nervousness?'

'Think of the horse.' said Alice. 'It's up to you to relax them. Being Arabs, they are prone to little hissy fits.'

'Hissy what's?' asked Geoff, intrigued.

'Being fretful is what it is. Keep working and I will tell you a little story about my own nervousness before a dressage test a few years ago when I was young and courageous.' He didn't know that she had been into dressage, and it can't have been all that long ago.

It was a hint as to how long she had been without her sight.

'Yep, I'm all ears,' said Geoff.

'Well, I used to belong to an adult horse-riding club which was wonderful fun. We would go on camps and sports days, gymkhanas and so forth. Anyway, I was very competitive in those days and had never done well in a dressage test. This day it was a day of instruction followed by a dressage test.

I went into my test, trotted down the side of the arena and I heard God speaking to me. My horse would always play up and spoilt any dressage test I had done in the past. God said, 'Forget about getting a ribbon. If you want her to have a nice relaxing day it's up to you to keep her calm and happy. Think of her well-being first, it's up to you. This amazed me and I realized that this was true. When I got competitive and tense, she would pick it up and she would be unhappy. O.K. God I said (to myself otherwise my club mates would be convinced of my weirdness). I will make her day enjoyable and we will forget about ribbons. My horse's peace of mind was my job.

We cruised through the dressage test beautifully and then we came to canter left in a circle. My usual reaction would have been 'Oh no I get she leads off the wrong leg which would be major points lost but this time I sat deep in the saddle shut my eyes and floated around the curve of the circle as if in a dream.

'Well done, that was a really good test!' my friend shouted.

'I know!' I shouted to her laughing a bit and stroking my horse's silky neck. My little mare wasn't sweating or chaffing at the bit. She walked out of that arena languidly, quite unlike her usual self.

At the end of the day the blue ribbon was presented to me. I had longed for a ribbon (of any colour) for years and now we had come first. That's the end of the story. I walked out of there and home to the paddock where I kept my horse in a cloud of glory and I had no doubt that God's words had made this day so wonderful.'

'It's pretty amazing Alice.' said Geoff adjusting the cheek strap of the bridle. He wouldn't put it on until it was time to ride but he was meticulous in his preparations and wanted his horse to be as comfortable as possible because it was a long way to go with uncomfortable gear. He didn't want to be causing irritation. Smithy just wouldn't travel well if he was in pain of any kind.

Alice's words had settled him right down and had switched his focus from winning to simply enjoying his journey through the bush. 'You've set my mind at ease actually,' said Geoff. 'Yes, you have. Hopefully both horses will be calm. They really are full of beans and I hope Smithy doesn't use up too much energy. He's the one I want to ride but if for some reason he is vetted out, then Parsley is my other option. It's hard keeping two horses fit. What if they both got vetted out?' said Geoff thinly veiling his hysteria.

'I'm sure they won't.' said Alice reassuringly.

'Parsley is a much calmer horse than Smithy but Smithy is the real talent when it comes to the endurance side of things.' said Geoff.

'You're in charge of both of them so you can decide how to keep them relaxed. I have every faith in you Geoff. These horses love you and trust you, don't you?' Alice stroked the two horses and gave them both a bit of carrot (the top of course because June would never let a good bit of food go to the animals that could be eaten by a person) which they snuffled up swiftly.

'Today was a real milestone. It was the best chance Geoff had to win the race he had competed in for six years. Both he and the horses were in for a long slog. Smithy and his spare horse Parsley walked obediently onto the float having long ago accepted their lot as beasts of burden.

Alice was outside while he made the last adjustment to the horse float and when he came up to say goodbye to her, she whispered 'I'll be praying for you'.

'Thank you. I'll need it.' he smiled.

'I'll pray you don't get knocked off by a branch and that none of your gear breaks, that Smithy stays full of energy and sensible and doesn't go lame. I want you to be safe and to enjoy the beauty of the bush you go through. Is that enough?' she asked somewhat breathlessly.

'It sounds fine to me!' said Geoff as he reached for her hand. '*You* cross my mind many times in a day!' Alice withdrew.

'Me? What do you think about me?' Curiosity was killing her.

'Mainly that you would fall in love with me.' he said. His honest face searched hers for some sign of real affection.

She put on her poker face. There was silence for a while. Alice sniffed, turned away and attempted to be casual and to ignore the comment but secretly thought *How do you know I haven't already?*

'Anyway, I can't let you go off and do something dangerous without telling you I care enough to pray for you. It's the least I can do. You're quite nice Geoff,' she smiled.

Geoff brushed a lock of hair from her forehead.

'Mm *quite* nice, am I? Wow, I wonder what that is on a scale of one to ten. I guess it's a step up from 'nice' and coming from you that is a major compliment.'

Alice smiled. She didn't want him to be ditched from his horse. At another time someone she loved went to his death and she had far from forgotten it.

'Watch out for branches, neck high one especially!'

He was glad she had told him this that she would pray for

him, but really wished she'd tell him she loved him. The only reason she had ever let him touch her was to be guided around from one place to another. Was she just very proud or was he actually repulsive to her *or* just plain unattractive? After all he did hang around with a lot of animals and probably stank. No that couldn't be it because she had already said she loved the smell of horses. *I'm always treading in some kind of manure, dog's the worst.* He checked his boots. *I know she likes me and I will just bide my time until she finds me totally irresistible. Which I am.* He smiled a bit of a swashbuckling smile then shook his head a bit disgusted with himself and carried on.

'Bye Alice,' he said fondly and squeezed her hand. He turned and walked to the four-wheel drive and drove away pulling the horse float. Smithy, gave a shrill whinny as they left the farm.

'Bye,' she said softly, giving a small wave and then gently clasping the hand he had touched.

The race started at ten which gave Geoff a couple of hours to settle and prepare. There would be vet checks along the way and everything had to be just so to keep Smithy powering on. Heart rate and other vital bodily functions had to be right.

Alice could imagine Smithy with his skinny nose dipping and lunging, as he climbed a steep hill. *I'll be at the finish, oh yes I will, and he will see me there. I hope he wins. This is one of his goals in life and he will do it well. Anyway, back to the farm and there's a lot of day to put in. I think June is cooking up a storm for the 'boys' and I have to be a part of it. Geoff would be happy with a pie or a sandwich along the way culminating in the big finale, June's huge Irish stew.*

Geoff's mother was fussing around in the kitchen. Technically it wasn't fussing but simply doing what came naturally. Her routine was always the same. After every cooking episode she would wash up and that the part Alice played. Then the dishes were put away which obviously June did. Then it would all start again, the cooking, then washing up, then putting away, and this was pretty much designed to put June's mind at ease but Alice found it baffling and neatness taken to ridiculous limits. She and Al had seen their son off earlier but Alice was afraid they may overhear her conversation with him, which was one of the reasons Alice whispered her prayer to Geoff. They had already said goodbye and wished him well because they knew he would need a little privacy to speak to Alice. This actually showed great restraint on June and Al's part, giving the young ones their space. *By golly, my son is a lovely boy, the best. I hope he thinks carefully who he wants as a life partner.* thought June to herself as she had watched Geoff and Alice saying goodbye near the horse float. *He is a catch and I'm sure Alice knows that. Oh, my how I worry about my boy! I want him to be happy and fulfilled in his life.* June was getting a little teary as she remembered Geoff as a little baby and then as a sweet demanding little toddler. *Hasn't changed much. And now he has degrees he's an accountant and I still get to do his washing. I must be an idiot, but he doesn't mind. And I have to the time.*

'It would have been nice to stay at the race all day.' said Alice wistfully.

170

'Why would you want to do that?' said June rather shocked.

'Well, I could have found something to do or eat while I waited at the finish line.' 'You can eat here dear, not a lot of food escapes these men but there is still plenty. And it's freezing outside! In a few minutes we can have a nice cup of tea and some jam roll. I know you like that one!' laughed June.

Alice would have preferred to stay there at the race all day but June had to cook a stew which it seemed needed at least two dedicated females on duty.

'Can I help?' she asked.

'Yes dear' replied June giving her a wooden spoon. 'Just keep stirring this till it thickens. June had added water to the corn flour and stirred it thoroughly. It had now been added to the thin liquid of the stew to make gravy. This required constant stirring to stop it sticking to the bottom of the pot and getting lumps. Alice was thinking about going back to the city, about how hard it would be after her taste of the bush again. It wouldn't be fair to hinder the whole family by outstaying her welcome. *But the smells of the eucalypts and the river, and sounds of the whip birds and the blue wrens are just intoxicating! How I'll miss them!* She felt homesick just thinking about leaving the bush behind. Yes, and Geoff.

June was talking as Alice came out of her daydream.

'Geoff will get food and drink on the way but I just want to give him a nice hot meal for tonight. You know what the men are like. Big eaters!'

'Yes they *are!*' agreed Alice. *But then again do they have any choice? Food is very important out here. Lovingly made, constantly made. There's no fast food here. It's slow food and it takes all day every day.*

He'll have a pie on the way hoe I'm sure, but he won't tell June. I just hope for his sake that he can muster up enough hunger to eat that stew. June will be so depressed if he doesn't eat it. The stew wasn't warm. It didn't seem to be cooking at all. Alice turned the hotplate up a little.

A few minutes later June shrieked and ran over to the stove.

'Oh Alice, couldn't you smell that? You turned on a hotplate and the hotplate cover is burning.'

'I'm, I'm sorry,' said Alice shrinking back. 'I couldn't feel the stew cooking so I turned...' She felt like saying to June: 'you should be grateful that your precious stew isn't what's burning!'

'The hot plate that the stew is on takes a while to heat up, it's always been that way,' said June saying each word with emphasis and a space between each as it reinforcing some information for a very small child.

She said to herself with irritation 'Oh no! The cover's burnt right through!' and to Alice she said 'Look, dear, go for a little fresh air, go on, I'll fix this up.' she had lifted the hot plate cover off with a knife.

Alice felt her face burning with shame. She went to her room and grabbed a handful of tissues which she felt certain she would need although part of her wanted to be strong and ignore the whole thing. But it did hurt. She wanted to make June happy with her but now she had blown it for all time or so it seemed right now.

'Yes, I *will* go and get some fresh air.' she muttered under her breath, 'some very fresh air,' tears rolled down her face. She had to get out, and away from June. She would simply die if June saw her like this. She had her pride. The last time she felt this humiliated was when she wet her pants at preschool a memorable day when some cruel children (as they say children can be so cruel) called out 'wet pants, wet pant' at her all the way to the gates of the school where her mother met her and yelled at the horrible children. As she recalled, the children ran off crying, a small punishment for their actions and less than they deserved. She never forgot that. This was definitely on par with that. She needed to be in the bush where nobody was disappointed with her or made her feel incompetent. Her already poor self-esteem was bruised and had reached an all-time low. *I bet my heart has slowed down. I think I am setting into stone. My heart is hurting. I am sad, yes sad, sad. I am getting out of here tout suite. Fancy ever thinking I could ever measure up to his parent's expectations! What a joke! Al was a nice man. How could he be married to her?'*

She went out of the garden gate and started to go down the paddock towards Geoff's mare and foal which was a long walk that would take her an hour least. She stumbled, ran and walked as fast as she could not wanting to be seen by the dreaded June. As she strode along Alice told herself that June was just a domestic drudge glorified to be pitied for the life she chose. Anger was speaking and she huffed and puffed out white clouds like the dragon she saw June as. *Who cared about a damned stew anyway? I wish I had burnt it now just to get to her. I'll go home tomorrow and never come back here. So much for country hospitality! Nobody ever mentions the Nazi Kitchen concentration camp but there you are, and here I am! Here in the twenty first century ruling the roost, matriarch June muscling in on me. Well, I won't let her get to me. I hope she won't see my me making my get away. Hurry, hurry feet and hands. There's the fence. Ooh watch out for the barbs, quickly!* The last time she had come down here she had Geoff's arm to guide her. Now she was on her own and a stick would have to suffice. On her right-hand side was the barbed wire fence running parallel to the track and she could always touch it with the stick to make sure she hadn't gone off course.

A bitter wind whipped around her face but the pain of her embarrassment and crushed spirit made her impervious to the cold. *How dare she treat me like that? Would I yell at her if she were blind and had burnt my precious hot plate cover?* Alice knew that it was time to let it go. Her outburst was over and she was thankful it hadn't been directed at June. *Geoff means too much to me to be rude to his mother. What is it with women, and not just country women but women in general? Do they have to metamorphose into anile androids?*

Let it go, let it go she breathed out. *Does it really matter anyway? I'm grateful that not to have June as a mother-in-law. Ha! That would be. a long and harsh sentence.* She blanked her mind out and tried to relax but the hurt was deep.

Through one gate and then another she went, slowly but surely. She wanted to reach the bush where all things were wild and nothing had to be anything, just itself. It was a long walk and she must have been gone for at least an hour. The weather had started to change, becoming very cold and splatters of rain sprayed her form timed to time as a gust hit her.

All around her the icy breeze buffeted her. Despite all of her will power and attempts at positive thinking, she was aching inside and it wasn't just June but a host of painful thoughts that were bleeding her dry.

She kept walking. The embarrassment of burning the hotplate cover was eating into her. *I just can't turn back to the house to face June (June the juggernaut)* thought Alice. 'Oh Lord,' she wept, 'I know it's a while since we really talked, but here I am and I feel so sad again.'

'I had so much advice for Geoff. Telling him how to ride. I can't even stir a pot of stew it seems. I want to be with him. I should have insisted that I stay out there at the race rather that lock horns with the lady of the house. Oh Geoff, who was I kidding? I need you now, so calm, so kind, so what I need right now. A lovely man, too good for me. I will be better. I now know that he loves me and would do anything for me. That is enough for me. But then again ouch there it goes again, the pain and the shame.

Tears rolled down her nose and dripped off. Out here she could actually speak out loud her very soul to God and to herself. She could talk out loud, and did. 'Please God take away the pain.

Please let me feel worthwhile. I'm not very nice. I know that, but you can make me good and kind and peaceful and happy. I am being drawn to you again because I just can't stay this way. But I don't want to burden Geoff. No, he has a bright future. To commit to me would be madness.'

'I'll definitely go home after today and settle down again in Melbourne. Everyone there is a bit depressed. I fit right in. Geoff can meet someone else and have a normal life. I just feel so sad and so bad.' she sobbed. Out here no one could hear her 'lose it' talking to no-one, or rather no one they could see. She was grateful for the moaning wind and the fresh smell of eucalypt trees. She felt like they were singing with her song of grief and carrying it away to the farthest reaches of the mountain country.

Her mind rattled on repetitiously, obsessively. She was making herself sick. *My first boyfriend, my betrothed, was taken in that abysmal, abseiling accident. He's gone. I thought I would never love anyone like that again and I would have been quite glad not to. If only I hadn't gone blind. Psychological cause or not it truly is a bummer. People have said to me, 'You weren't the cause of his death. I know that. But they don't understand. That isn't the point. The point is that I wasn't there with that lovely boy when he breathed his last, and I wanted to be there.*

Can't dumb people understand that?! Mum and Dad tried to help but I didn't want to go live with them. I needed to grieve alone. Jacquie would say I haven't done that either. She would say I've been a pathetic piner, depressing everyone I meet. She has been pairing me up with men for a while now and I wouldn't do it. Not that I hate men, but I honestly didn't think I would find one to measure up to Stephen. But now there is Geoff, the best surprise of my life.

It never really worried me before but now I've met a lovely man who loves me and…I don't want to be blind! I want Geoff's parents to think I'm fit for him, not some helpless child.

In spite of herself she gave a grim smile, thinking of the burnt hot plate cover and the work June would have scrubbing the blackness off it, or she might just toss the whole set of stove covers away. She wished she had burnt the stew, (which was the point of June's whole day) creating something really acrid to match her acrimonious feelings towards June and something really hard to clean up. *Just stop it, Alice! June's a darn good cook. Her best quality of course – and I'm not going to whinge about her anymore. She is Geoff's mother and she loves him too. We may have to share him and after all I'm not married to him. If I was there would probably be a few show downs but he's not mine.*

'Oh, why did I do that stupid thing and burn the hot plate cover! I'll never live it down.' *Geoff is out there riding through the bush totally unaware of the friction going with June, dumb man.* Alice laughed through her tears. *The kitchen drama may not even be affecting June. In her eyes I and Geoff are nothing but big children and I suppose she feels it's her right and her place to speak to me like that. The saying about wives being: 'in the kitchen via the bedroom' surely wouldn't apply to June. Where would she find the time for the bedroom after these extraordinary meals are accomplished?*

'Now I'm being silly' she almost spat. 'But no! She was really mean to me and it's all welling up again like a king tidal wave.' *They don't like me. I did want them to respect me as a person. Al's alright. I bet June can't wait till I go back to Melbourne. She probably wants a University Graduate for her son with twenty-twenty vision of course. Someone from Toorak with a bit of a plum in the mouth accent.*

She was wavering between hatred for them and extreme sadness. *I know that it's not really them that are the problem. It's me, stubborn, nasty me! I just want to be happy again. I can't bring Stephen back but I can live on in a way to make him proud of me. Why does Geoff have to be so obsessed with me, wanting to be with me for always? I feel a warm glow when I think of him, then I feel sad. Would he still like me I if I told him about the accident? I think I love him, No, not you Stephen, not anymore in this world. But Geoff. He is the one I love and I will not let him down, in this world. I want to let go of all of this bitterness. It's not fair to be so angry with his mother. She only wants the best for her son. I can understand that. All the anger I have for myself I'm pushing onto June and anyone else that crosses me. I've lost hope of ever seeing. If I ever got my sight back then I'd be a whole person again. If only. Even if I did have my sight, I bet I still would have burnt the blinking hot plate cover!*

She stopped her fast trudging to catch her breath. She shivered as the wind found its way through the hem of her jacket and anywhere her skin showed. She sighed wearily as she saw in her imagination her days in the Melbourne sheltered workshop stretching out in front of her, long and dark. Melbourne had that effect on people even if they weren't blind, she laughed callously.

The good thing was that Winter was long and cold and practically dark under a lot of clouds.

Picking up her pace she kept walking towards the horse paddocks.

It had been nice to be made much of by Geoff but enough was enough. She knew what Jacquie would say: (totally sick of her gloom) 'Just get over yourself, and grab that lovely guy while you have the chance!' Alice knew that was true but oh how hard it was to let these things go. Alice still wanted revenge. *Yes, I am a nasty piece of work, a wrathful retentive. What is this in my head that talks? The Oxford English Dictionary? Give it a rest Alice Are you an Oxford Graduate? This cold is freezing your brain! Big words don't become you.*

I'm better off being somewhere that caters for my handicap. Imagine if I was living in the country? Imagine another debacle with a hot plate cover and it could occur in my own house and next time I could burn the house down. It was only because I wasn't familiar with June's stove (that's my story anyway). Well anyway how could I have children and keep track of them? The dream about having children – it's childish and impossible. She was exhausted from her hysterical thoughts and sat down to rest pulling the collar of her coat around her neck. She sat as the cold air whipped across her face and she felt a string of cold ice particles, snow.

Deep within her a warning signal went off when she realised that she could actually die out here, alone in the snow, just a small bump hidden till the thaw. *Don't people get hypothermia in the snow and take of all their clothes 'cause they think they are too hot, and slur like a drunk? This is becoming serious. I think I am in serious trouble now and I don't really know. It's quite nice actually, curled up here.*

Suddenly more than anything else she wanted to live. A stab of shock went through her heart as she remembered how Geoff had squeezed her hand as he had said goodbye before he went to the race and that she had not responded in kind. *It would be too cruel for him to find me out here frozen and dead, in early Spring, possibly mummified. How can I be so flippant at a time like this? Oh, Geoff I really do love you and I would do anything to see you now. I must get back to the house. It's so cold…but it's nice here…Mmm, I think a short nap might help revive me.*

She just had to tell Geoff she loved him and loved him dearly.

Suddenly, there came a high distressed whinny somewhere close. Alice felt along the wire of the fence and snagged herself a couple of times. 'Ouch!' she exclaimed. 'Oh, it's you Carla', said Alice softly reassuring her for the mare was clearly upset and was making urgent *hoo, hoo, hoo* noises from her throat and through her nostrils as if saying 'help me please!'

'So that's the problem,' sighed Alice as she felt around the body of the foal and figured out just how tangled it was. Inwardly she tensed and started to panic, but knew that Carla needed her to be calm. After all she had preached that to Geoff that he had to be calm for his horse's well-being. If she panicked, the mare would sense this and the foal would be at the mercy of unforgiving barbed wire. The foal was in a curious sitting position on the top wire. How had he done this?

'It's alright Carla, just relax, haven't you got a silly foal!?' Carla calmed down as Alice stroked her velvet neck. Alice felt the foal's rump as it sat on the wire. It didn't struggle. The clever little thing sat quietly – although trembling and Alice knew it must be in pain as the barbs pricked the underside of its rump. The foal knew that its human friend was trying to help.

Ever so gently she eased up the hind quarters up until she was lifting the foal off the wire. With all the strength she possessed she heaved the foal up and off the barbed wire. She was so relieved that the foal came lose and that none of the barbs stuck or ripped into its little hide. She heard it fall with a thump onto the ground and hoped for the best.

Broken legs were a possibility she daren't even imagine. Her throat was dry and she couldn't swallow.

'Sorry about that little fella,' she rasped, 'but it had to be done. Please get up and walk.

You'll survive!'

She felt the foal shaking. It was so glad to be free of those sharp snagging barbs and his mother covering him with concerned little caresses, with her gentle quivering muzzle. The foal came over to Alice and gave a shrill whinny then sniffed her hand before prancing away. By the sound of its feet, it had four good ones and Alice breathed it seemed for the first time. *What a relief. I will never feel sorry for myself again. Geoff loves this little fellow and I am so glad I was here to save him. Thanks God!* Alice almost jumped back hearing herself speak his name. *Yes, thank you! My griping is officially at an end – well for a while at least!*

'Oh dear, you may need stitches little fella. I must get back to the house so a vet can check you out.' Alice started to retrace her steps but everything seemed unfamiliar and very cold. Her legs wouldn't go any faster even though she was pushing them a long at what seemed top speed.

She was fading fast and hadn't counted on such a debilitating cold which held her in its grip. Stinging granules took the warmth from her face. It pushed against her was in her mouth. Her coat buffeted like a sail. Where was soaking warmth? Aunty Linda's wood oven. Mmm, what a nice thought that was, to be in the kitchen with her cat and scones and date scones at that, *'beautiful'*.

Alice found shelter beside a large lichen covered rock and pulled her parka hood over her head. What I really need now is another Parker – a Geoff Parker and also another parker! Now she felt very tired and giggled as she drifted off into a deep sleep. *Nothing like a wood oven.* She would gladly stay here definitely for an hour or two. *Just a little nap to soak in this delicious warmth.*

As she drifted into a deep dark sleep, she began to dream. The wind picked up, and the temperature had fallen even further as it began to snow. Alice wept real tears in her sleep, as the mean thoughts that she had harboured towards Geoff's mother rose before her. In her dreams, she saw that woman bustling around her kitchen, faithfully serving her men-folk too much food, with no idea that she was so boring and interfering. Alice felt shame of her ugly feelings. It almost made her physically sick. The person she loved was Geoff, and June was his mother. She couldn't hate the one and love the other. They were family and she was an outsider. *June loved her* son (she kept saying and thinking it and was gradually really starting to believe it). *You would never blame a horse for defending its foal or a cat defending its kitten, or a dog defending its pup...Shut up Alice! But seriously.*

Why should the mother want to give him to a sulky disabled girl?

In her mind she saw Jesus holding out his loving nail scarred hands to her, saying: 'I love you just the way you are and I will fix your problems, don't worry.' Then he said 'Geoff loves you just the way you are.'

Yes, He does love me! she thought with excitement She had all along been so obsessed with her own jockeying monkeys to realise what a gift Geoff was, a gift from God. Jesus had also given his life for her own bitter and twisted one...to make her well. If she was happy inside, that would be the wellness she truly needed and yearned for.

In her mind's eye, she handed it over, all he broken dreams, the bitterness, anger and grief. 'Please fix it all, Jesus.' she wept.

She felt her demons fading and she was ready to make things right that could be righted. Gratitude and joy welled up in her as tears burst fresh tracks down her face. God had become real to her again and she would never be the same again. He was alive in her heart, a friend who would never desert her. She felt sheltered by giant wings despite the falling sleet. Alice was at the end of herself now, exhausted and drifting between sleep and wakefulness, losing consciousness. *This must be what it's like to be a chicken* she thought with a contented smile.

Eleven

Geoff had judged his ride well, not pushing his Arab gelding Smithy too hard. The months of training had made the difference. The plucky little horse trotted to the finish line head and tail held high. Geoff was tired, and all he could think about was seeing Alice. She would be so proud of him. In a blur of cameras and splashing champagne they came through the tape.

Geoff glanced around but couldn't see his beloved fragile Alice. His parents rushed up. 'She's gone. We had a bit of a fight,' blurted June dabbing her hanky to her stinging teary eyes. 'She burnt a hot plate cover and I lashed out. I didn't mean to upset her.' 'Hot-plate cover? What the? What do you mean lashed out? Geoff, grabbed his mother by the shoulders, something he had never ever done except when he was joking with her in the kitchen. 'Where is she now?'

'It's alright son,' said Al more reassuringly than he felt. 'We've called Search and Rescue into find her, but' he said, unable to hide his fears 'she went walking and...it's snowing our way.'

Geoff looked like a red pressure cooker about to blow. 'Snowing! My God, so you just let her go out?'

'No darling.' said the stricken June. 'We didn't realize she had gone for some time, and it wasn't snowing when she left. I didn't think she would leave the house. I thought she had gone to her room. I thought it best to leave her alone for a while.' June was suffering for her mistake. She had no doubts now just how much her son felt for Alice, and she wished she had been more patient in the kitchen. If Alice was hurt, she could never cook a scone again. It would be a mockery of her role of a nurturing mother. Geoff handed his horse to one of the vets who was doing the final physical examination to see whether it had arrived fit and well. One of the officials was a friend of Geoff's and agreed to float the horse home for him.

'Thanks a million mate!' exclaimed Geoff.

'No worries, mate.' Came his friend's reply. 'But don't you want to wait a bit to see if you've won?' he said, not knowing the full extent of why Geoff had to go so immediately.

'No offense but I don't give a rat's!' yelled Geoff, as he took off at a run to the four-wheel drive.

Geoff leapt into the car, roaring off, his parents sitting grimly and silently in the back. In a half an hour that seemed like an eternity to Geoff, they rolled through the gates of the property. The search and rescue teams dotted the snow covered paddocks their torches and headlights tunnels of light battling the darkening sky. Geoff strode relentlessly through one paddock then to the next. Fear almost choked him and tears threatened to burst from his eyes. 'I can't lose you! Alice you're so *precious* to me!' He clenched his teeth and his hands. *Why couldn't you have been happy knowing that? You can't hurt yourself, surely not over a stupid hot plate cover!* He was sweating, yet his breath came out in steamy clouds through the cold air. Snow fell heavily and in smothering clouds.

Geoff was furious with his mother for upsetting Alice in the kitchen but also knew that Alice was quite easily upset. He spoke out loud and as he strode on. 'I'm coming. I won't let you harm yourself little darling.' He loved her fiercely. If he found her alive, he wouldn't take no for an answer when he asked for her to marry him. 'She needs someone to take care of her, silly worrying girl. My poor girl, may you never leave me again and I will look after you so well!' Geoff scanned around bur it was getting dark and snow was covering everything. He pushed himself, panting and sweating, staring all around starting to panic. *Where is she!? Why is she so easily crushed?* he wondered then speculated, *Because she's blind? There's more to it than that. She can be so sweet and funny yet today and she was sweet before the race. Not exactly affectionate but something like it.* He found a trail of blood in the snow. His stomach convulsed and he felt faint. It led to the foal. He exhaled and held his for head in relief. The gentle little creature was trembling with a gash in its hind quarters. There were traces of hair and skin on the top strand of barbs. *Alice!* He thought in excitement. She might have lifted it off the top wire! She must be close!

He looked around desperately, helplessly. Searchers must have covered every inch of the paddock. Geoff focused on a gully and a small rocky outcrop almost completely covered in snow. He ran and stumbled along and saw a patch of blue in the white ice building up beside the rock. He tore off the snow.

'Alice!' He clutched her to himself then cried out hoarsely: 'She's here!'

The searchers crowded around and a paramedic checked her pulse. 'She's alive! She's got hypothermia. Get her out of these wet clothes, you too and get warm now!' Once in the ambulance the medico continued his volley of instructions. 'She's got to be warmed up, come on man!' Geoff nodded, stripped off his coat and boots in seconds and pulled a thermal eiderdown over both of them. Alice was in a flannelette blanket followed by another foil blanket designed to bring up her core temperature. Geoff pushed strands of damp hair away from her face. His own cheek was damp with melted snow and warm rivulets of tears as he gazed at her as if she were to the most valuable jewel every discovered, and she was to him.

'Alice, you shouldn't have wandered off in this snow,' he scolded her gently, his voice cracking. 'You mustn't go! I need you!' Geoff kissed her blue lips tenderly, as if pleading life back into her. She weakly pushed against him, whispering 'No! Leave me alone.' and then lapsed back into unconsciousness. Geoff stroked her face and tried to give her his warmth.

On the ride in the ambulance Geoff had time to think. He couldn't imagine a life without her. She made him laugh, she made him cringe, she made him cry. Yes, cry and he would not be happy until she was giving him cheek again. Her dear soft face he would love to kiss but he couldn't force her to love him. *Oh Lord, bless this little girl and bring her to my side. I will never leave her.*

188

Just lying beside her was like a fulfillment of his dreams. To be so close to her. He would not take advantage of the situation and her helplessness. He would respect her wish to 'be left alone'. But he had to move the wet locks of her hair off her face.

Twelve

Alice had been in a coma for several days. Geoff, ashen faced, sat by her bedside during the entire time. He held her hand and stroked her forehead. His eyes were sore from crying and indeed he felt drained. He scanned her face constantly for signs of movement, eyelids fluttering, anything. This kind of pain was new to him as he had never had a loved one as incapacitated as this. He kept wishing over and over that he was there in the kitchen when the fracas had occurred. *And they say animals can be territorial!'*

How could he have left her in that kitchen? After all, the kitchen was his mother's domain, her territory and she marked it with various small rules about where hand towels and tea towels were located, about the arrangement of kitchen utensils. In other words, all was in order, her order – June's world order. Geoff was starting to see the picture from Alice's point of view. He had heard of the one kitchen one woman rule but had always thought it to be a myth spread by men. This time they were right.

Now that he thought back over the past week, he recalled various things his mother had said.

'No dear I leave the salt on the table'…'The hand towels are inside the pantry and the tea towels are on the rack'…'Don't you know the difference between hand towels and tea towels? The hand towels have the looped pile, the tea towels are linen.'…'No dear, just leave the toaster on six because I always cook crumpets Thursday morning.'…and so it went on. Alice did her best, but even the best would never be enough for his mother. *But that's the way it is. It's a separate country, culture which Alice was not aware of. Despite the clash, they fed the chooks together quite happily. There's not a lot of technique to feeding chooks and subsequently not many rules.* Geoff shook his head sadly. His dad had not stood up to his mum the way he should have, and she had not built him up the way a wife should have (except in the food department), scorning his 'Dad' jokes.

Treating him like a child, Dad was good but he had definitely kowtowed to June. Geoff thought - he would love to have words with his mum, but now was not the time and hospital was certainly not the place.

He looked at his heart's desire and his heartache, Alice lying so still.

'Come on Alice, I'm here, don't leave me. We can be happy…we can…just come back to me!' he said, for what felt like the millionth time. He pressed his face into her hand and kissed it fervently. Tears rolled freely from his eyes. *Just how many tears can one man have? A while ago I would have said none because I've never really cried before – not that I can remember. But now…I've only known her such a short while, but I want to spend a lifetime with her no matter what happens. She wouldn't be in this position if I hadn't pleaded with her to come with me to the farm. Yes,* he thought knowing he was taking a leaf from Alice's books. *It's all my fault! She thinks everything is her fault. 'Except when it's yours.' she would say, with that cheeky look on her face.*

The hospital was an old one made of red clay brick and white painted window frames in small lattice pattern. It was cold outside, but every so often a shaft of white golden sunlight would stream into the room and across her bed. *Too cold to ride outside. I've done enough riding for the time being.* Geoff thought of the champagne flowing when he had won the endurance race, which he hadn't even collected his trophy for. He was amazed by things he had thought were such world stopping events in his life that were now, unimportant. He wanted his girl to come around in more ways that than one. He didn't care if she didn't love him. He just wanted her back, back in the land of the living. Back with a quick quip or even a petulant toss of the head. Geoff was bereft and wondered when or if he was ever going to see his dear girl open her eyes again.

'I can read your mind.' said Al, placing his hand on Geoff's shoulder. 'Don't try to solve the problems of the world here and now. People are the way people are and they hurt one another all the time. Your mum feels shocking about the whole thing and is too afraid to see you. I know she can be a trouble maker but there is a still a very good and kind side to her.'

'I know dad. just wish she could have not been herself while Alice was staying here.

Couldn't she have put on some kind of neutral act, and not

stirred Alice up?'

'Come and have a cup of tea.' said Al placing his hand on Geoff's shoulder.

'I don't want to leave her Dad, what if...'

'No what ifs,' said Al firmly. 'What good will you be to her if you're a zombie like this?' 'Duh, don't know dad. You're cheering me up.' said Geoff with a glazed stare.

'It's alright Geoff,' said the nurse. 'It's my turn to worry about her and I get paid for it!' Geoff looked at her with amused disbelief thinking how tactless and politically incorrect she was, but he liked it. She smirked and carried on with her work, tending to Alice while Geoff went out for a cup of tea and a sandwich with his parents.

The cafeteria was quite busy and cheerful but June was especially grey looking, feeling a load of guilt on her shoulders for what had happened. She spoke hesitantly and with a bit of a quaver in her voice: 'We've contacted Alice's parent in Queensland and they are coming down straight away. They told us a few things about her that she kept hidden from us, not that I am having a go at her,' she insisted.

'You wouldn't want to be mum,' said Geoff darkly.

Geoff listened intently as June related Alice's story, of the abseiling death of her fiancée and Alice's subsequent blindness.

'Apparently, she never forgave herself for not being there the day of the accident, and went blind from shock.

'Blind from shock? How does that even happen? Is that true?

Can that really happen?' 'She was apparently so distraught, and very devoted to her fiancée but dear...but you broke through her barriers. She loves you.' June smiled and squeezed her son's hand. Geoff was silent as he drank his cup of tea. His parents looked at him and at each other with concern. Al put his hand on Geoff's hand.

Geoff thought to himself: *Yes, I think she might love me, even though she hasn't really shown it, I just wish she'd come back. And I would know for sure what the score is. At any rate just to have her back whether she is for me or not is not the question. I should have been more obvious but I was afraid she'd run a mile if I was too keen.'*

Geoff said to his parents, 'I want her well. I want her to be happy. Whether that is with me or not.'

Al gulped and winced. 'Why wouldn't she love you?!' exclaimed June. 'I think you are absolutely gorgeous darling!'

'Mum, this is not the time or place. When I was four years old was probably the time to say such things, not now. It's a trifle sickening.'

'I'm sorry.' said June downcast. 'But what mother doesn't adore her boy?'

'Mum!' said Geoff not prepared to speak any more on the subject.

Meanwhile Alice's room was silent and the nurse had gone out for a moment. Alice's eyelids fluttered open and she stared with a mixture of confusion and fear at a bright shaft of light from the window thinking. *So, this is it, heaven, wow! I made it. No, I'm not.*

She heard doctors in the corridor talking, and realised that she was still on planet earth. *To herself she squealed and giggled. I can see! For a moment she had no idea where she was, but then memories flooded back to her, the snowy field, the fight with June, rescuing the foal from the barbed wire fence, more snow, and then falling asleep It was cold, so cold. And then, she remembered flashing lights, being held in Geoff's embrace – he had kissed her! And then – oblivion.*

She heard the nurses. She must be in hospital; she had figured that out. Quickly she shut her eyes again. She didn't want the nurses to know right away that she was awake. And she hoped beyond hoped that Geoff was there somewhere. She longed to give him a wonderful surprise.

Geoff walked back to the door of her room. Alice had sneaked a peek and saw his parents leave. She now pretended to be still asleep. Geoff sat beside her sadly and lay his head in the curve of her waist. Gently she drew her arm out of the sheets and placed her hand on his head. He started as if he had just been electrocuted by an electric cattle prod, his eyes wild and his guts wrenched within him. Her blue eyes gazed directly at him, more beautiful and deep than he ever remembered.

'Geoff, isn't it?' she smiled and her eyes lit up with warmth. He fell on her, embraced her in the hospital bed and wept, shaking with big sobs.

'I thought you would never come back to me!' he gasped as he wet her cheeks with his man tears which were wetter and more meaningful than woman tears (something that Alice had teasingly said to him once.)

With fake trepidation she then said, 'Yes, you're not too bad looking I suppose...' 'Lucky for you I'm from good looking stock!' he answered in a husky voice, vocal cords tight with emotion. He was laughing but tears kept welling up in his eyes. He felt like choking her and kissing her at the same time.

Then suddenly he realized what she had said. Geoff could say nothing but shake his head as he couldn't believe it. 'I thought you'd never wake up.' His hands shook and his face twitched with emotions he was just keeping in check. 'But I prayed to God. Oh my God did I pray!' He gave a little laugh and her soft hand wiped away a tear from his trembling face. With that Geoff unashamedly lifted his head and looked up and said, 'Thank so much God. I'll never thank you enough if I live to be three hundred.' She shut her eyes and traced her hand over his face and said gently teasing: 'Actually I think you *felt* better looking.'

'You can't get away with this flirting anymore.' said Geoff grabbing her wrists in a grip of delighted amusement and love and planted a tender kiss right on her mouth. 'So assertive Geoff!' said Alice. Her eyes sparkled and she gave a giggle then she gazed into his eyes. 'I wanted you so much. I couldn't leave you behind because...because... I couldn't stand you crying and...' she hesitated then slowly said what was so hard for her to finish saying, 'You see I love you, more than you'll ever know.'

Geoff sat quietly with his hands cupping her face as if he were holding a day-old baby chicken. 'Even if you show it in strange ways.'

Now it was her turn to cry. She wrapped her arms around Geoff and just loved the smell of him. 'Don't *ever* go away and don't *ever* take that jumper off. I love the smell of it. It's the smell of *you*. You were so hurt when I rejected you. I had to come back to tell you that I loved you and I think I loved you the first time I met you at Jacquie's on the verandah.'

'Really?' Geoff arched an eyebrow at her in scepticism.

'You smelt like horses and I love horses.' said Alice with an amused smile as she watched him squirm.

'It's a *nice* smell!" she laughed.

'No amount of washing can get rid of it then?' he queried.

'No amount of washing I'm afraid. Just do what the horses do to get clean. Roll in the dirt!' She beamed at him. At that moment he couldn't stand to be so close and not touch her. His eyes became dark with deep longing.

'You've got a funny look in your eyes and your lip is pointed.' she said mocking him again.

'Oh, have I?' he laughed. A huge smile lit up his face. Then he got serious again. 'I'll cherish you forever.' She could feel his breath and his mouth moved close to hers and was drawn with a kind of magnetism. He could feel her trembling like a nervous deer. As their lips met Alice floated like a dove upwards towards the light. She was dizzy and desired him so much. Her soul had joined with his, in this beautiful kiss. His hand held her face tenderly then stroked her hospital hair which was a little tangled and fluffy at the back. He didn't care and he grasped her to himself but not in a rough way. He felt he would like to gently crush her.

The nurse walked in and Alice glanced up and stared at her directly in the eyes. The nurse gave a scream and dropped her linen and medications. Geoff helped pick up the dropped things while the nurse had run off to find a doctor.

Alice watched Geoff. The love that she had saved for Stephen flowed to Geoff and she was released at last from memories of the past. Most of the doctors in the hospital (which was a country one) came to view the miracle girl. Despite being made a huge fuss of, Alice was too happy to care and took all of the attention in her stride. After all, she had kissed a beautiful man who adored her.

Alice's parents arrived in due course and met Geoff's parents. The double joy of seeing their daughter alive and well and with sight was almost too much for them. In fact, Alice asked that they not be told of her sight so she could surprise them. What a surprise that was! She jumped out of bed and ran up to hug her mother. Her mother almost fainted and her father staggered back, eyes popping with incredulity.

'Darling I'm so happy for you, faintingly happy!' laughed her mother after she had recovered in a chair fanning herself with her hand. Geoff is a really nice young fellow and only has eyes for you, that's for sure!'

'Mum! careful he might hear.'

'What would be the problem with that?' she asked.

'I don't want him to think I'm needy or that I'm so keen for heaven's sake.'

'And what would the problem be with that?'

At that moment Geoff walked into her room. 'Good day Geoff!' said her father, offering Geoff a chair. You and your parents have really made Alice happy. And she can see. It's all thanks to you.'

'Well, hardly.' said Geoff eyes averting in embarrassment.

Alice rolled her eyes feeling the same way. 'Excuse me!' she said imperiously. 'You're talking about me and I'm right here. I'm not a helpless wreck!'

'Of course, you aren't, but you have been blessed sweetie,' said her father patting her forehead and stroking her hair back. 'You know I'm right!'

'Of course, you are dad, you always are!' she sighed flopping back onto her pillow. 'Yes, I am grateful to everyone for not letting me freeze out in the paddock because I've inadvertently gotten my sight back through it.'

Geoff smiled. 'She saved a foal that was stuck on the fence. No small thing and I reckon she's just about capable of anything.' He fondly patted her leg and gazed at her in adoration.

'Yes, she did well and we're all proud of her,' said Geoff to Alice's father.

Mum looks as though she's on some kind of happy pills. The way she's staring and smiling is just not natural! I suppose she is just happy to see me well and seeing. She reminds me of myself at Christmas time when I got my rocking horse and just about had to be surgically removed from it. Geoff has that bright yet glazed look about him and heck he's good looking. I took him to be some kind of nerd and this is a pleasant surprise.

Alice's dad and Geoff stayed when the doctor came to see her. She couldn't make the doctor see that she was one hundred percent well. Despite feeling great and capable of anything she was confined to bed and told to not to get up for a few days.

Later Geoff heard her arguing with the nurse, 'Forget that delicate rubbish. I jumped out of bed and ran over to my mum you know?!'

'And *she* fainted!' snapped the nurse.

'Next time it will be you with a broken bone for your trouble. Now you stay there or I will send the doctor around – or maybe several doctors – to have words with you. I know it's exciting getting your sight back and everything but one nasty fall and you could lose it again. Does this compute to you?' The nurse gave a wistful smile and said, 'It *is* exciting. Believe me I think this is nothing short of a miracle young lady. I am not an old sour puss nurse for the fun of it I just have to draw the line at what is not safe for you. They don't call me the enforcer for nothing.' she said as she left the room.

June came to visit Alice by herself without Al and looked decidedly edgy.

'I'm sorry!' said June…'No I'm sorry!' they blurted together. Both laughed nervously and looked around the room. June grasped Alice's hand and patted it. 'I was sick with worry.' June's tears, which were hard to come by for her, rolled to her cheeks, but she wiped them away quickly with a hanky. She couldn't remember the last time she cried. 'Alice, I've decided that the men came can cook their own meals occasionally and help around the house. I have become so obsessed with household that I don't have any hobbies of my own, cooking and cleaning being the only ones! (I know, it's sick.) I was jealous of you and Geoff going riding in the bush. I haven't so much as gone for a walk to the end of the paddock in years. I would like you to take me under your wing – (even though you are a spring chicken) when you're well enough – and show me how to have fun because all I seem to be is a tough old boiler and a nagging one at that! To think I might have been the one to cause Geoff to lose the one he has waited for all his life.' She grasped both Alice's hands and squeezed them fondly. 'I will be your friend Alice, if you want to be mine. I have been told I can be quite funny on occasion. I certainly can be sarcastic.' Alice went to disagree (even if this would be dishonest). She really didn't get any pleasure out of June's pain and wanted to stop it.

'No dear!' said June raising her hand. 'It's true. Anyway, I'm off now. I know I said that boys can cook for themselves occasionally but this is not the occasion. We're getting fish and chips!' she laughed triumphantly.

'Well, you enjoy them!' said Alice, giving June a little hug and kiss goodbye. June looked back and waved, a winsome girlish happy smile on her face.

It was nice to see June happy. Underneath Alice's judgmental attitude for others, she was an even harsher judge of herself. Now that she was happier in her life, the lives of others would benefit.

A few days went by, and the doctor said that Geoff could take Alice for a walk outside.

He lifted her up off the bed and gently placed her in the wheelchair putting a warm blanket over her knees (and a shawl his mother had given to him for Alice) around her shoulders. Alice was touched by this tender care. As he wheeled her along the verandah of the hospital they talked.

'I don't know how you put up with me,' said Alice. 'I hardly let you hold my hand. These days most guys wouldn't persist if they couldn't get to home base in about three dates! – So I've heard!' she said to make sure he didn't think she was such a girl. He would know that from his experience with her. She smiled. *Miss Beluga the white whale who lives in the arctic waters, never to be tampered with, that's me!* She snickered to herself and got up quite a giggle.

Geoff wondered what she was laughing about but just let it go. He didn't like the sound of it because it was about him no doubt.

'I guess it must be more than a physical attraction that I have for you then.' he laughed. 'Oh, Geoff that makes me feel so much better knowing I'm not attractive to you. It's my intellect you like, hey?'

'Hardly!' he laughed 'Don't be ridiculous!'

'So now I'm not pretty and I'm stupid as well.'

'Don't be silly! You *are* very pretty but you could show more finesse.' But there was more. His voice dropped and became warm and husky. 'I loved you from the start with your stubborn way and the way you love that stupid cat! It gave me hope that one day you would love me the way you loved it.'

Alice froze for a moment. Tabby! How could she forget her precious companion!

'W…where is Tabby? He must be going crazy without me!'

Geoff 'shushed' her, 'It's OK.' he soothed. 'Tabby and my dad have become rather good friends. He now finds my dad's lap his favourite spot. And he sleeps on the end of my parent's bed.'

Alice relaxed. 'Oh, I'm so relieved. Really? Your dad and Tabby? That's so cute. And what's wrong with loving a cat? You know I knew him before I had ever smelt your jumper (which was your main attraction).' To this Geoff could only shake his head and smile.

Alice raised her chin beckoning for a kiss while at the same time being positively insolent. It didn't go unnoticed by the man who had longed for her for so long.

'Ooh my neck!' said Alice with a giggle.

'Sorry darling.' said Geoff who was now crouching next to the wheel chair, more at her height.

'Is that better?' he said gazing directly and adoringly into her eyes then, 'Are you OK?' 'I am very OK. Geoff, you are a lovely man! I just had a stiff neck. You just had to stoop to my level and there's nothing wrong with that!' she said saucily as Geoff encompassed her mouth cutting off her rude comment and their breath became one.

Pointing to the mountains Geoff said: 'That can be our home if you want it to be. He stroked her hair. I'll give you what just about every girl at some time in her life has wanted.'

'What?' asked Alice loudly and with some suspicion.

'A horse. And not just any horse but one that you can practically dress up in dolls clothes.'

'You mean a nice quiet horse that I can brush and plait and paint (its hooves that is).'

'Yep, a horse like you had years ago. Now, will you marry me?'

'How can I say no after that?' laughed Alice clutching his hand and then did a very tender very un-Alice like thing. She pressed her lips onto the top of his hand and gave a little sob.

With that hand Geoff stroked her face kissed her soft cheek.

She threw her arms around his sobbed into his chest.

Alice again reached for his hand. It was rough-palmed but so beautiful and delicate on top. How she loved that hand, for that was all she had known of him for so long.

Geoff looked at his beautiful gift, his Alice, who was alive and gazing into the sunset. Alice spoke softly, 'It wasn't just chance that had saved my life, and gave my sight back.' 'I know,' said Geoff looking deeply into her eyes.' The Lord's been good to us.' he said. 'Take me off the most desperate bachelors list. He knelt and held her hand. Be my wife little fella.'

'Yes!' laughed Alice 'But I'll kill you with kindness, you know that!'

'You mean with your cooking. I wouldn't want you to go to all that trouble.' said Geoff teasingly.

'Yeah, yeah! I really can cook you know. Don't you dare cringe at the thought! Be nice to me Geoff or when I burn toast or the roast, I'll leave home!

'And go for a walk to the North Pole no doubt.'

On the outside Geoff laughed but was thinking to himself how close to complete disaster all of this had been. All he felt now was gratitude and joy. On top of it all he now had a perfect little partner who he could tease all his life and really enjoy it. Could she stand it though?

Alice stared long and hard at Geoff's face and saw his perfectly kissable lips. She leant over and placed the tenderest of pecks on them then lowered her gaze a little embarrassed by her forwardness. He gently tilted her chin up and kissed her eyes one then another.

'I love you. You come here little mouse deer.'

Alice remembered the mouse deer story of when he patted a timid little mouse deer in a Singapore zoo. It was quite a cute thing to say.

No more would she pull away. That kiss was something. This mouse deer wouldn't disappear into the jungle. She trembled. She was timid but she felt his love reach her and was glad it had taken time. But no, she would never pull away again.

Epilogue

Geoff and Alice were married in the Spring, under the eucalyptus trees near Geoff's home. Jacquie was Alice's maid of honour. They made their home in a newly built house on Geoff's family's property. Geoff took over the management of the farm from his father. They made frequent trips to Melbourne for stock sales and business, so Alice never lost touch with Jacquie. Alice's parents sold up their banana farm, and moved down to the high country so that they could live nearby. After three years, Geoff and Alice welcomed their first baby girl, Amelia. Eighteen months later, they welcomed another daughter, Anabelle. Two years later they had twin boys, Stephen and Geoffrey. Alice and June became firm friends, and June taught Alice how to make scones – better than her sister Linda's – while Alice reminded June of how to have fun in her life. At present, Alice helps Geoff in the running of their farm, in the livestock management, including the horses, and loves looking after her family and children. Alice lives her life to the fullest, never looking back to her old life or dark days in Melbourne.

Margot La Fontaine

*Artist and writer who enjoys the ridiculous and equally the profound,
who loves romance, nature and the Australian High Country.*

© 2021 Margot La Fontaine

Produced and published by Margot La Fontaine

All rights reserved

Cover painting by Margot La Fontaine

Design by: David Potter
www.transformer.com.au

Edited by: Amanda Proos

Printed and distributed by Ingram Spark
www.ingramspark.com

First edition 2021

ISBN 978-0-646-85382-6 (pbk)
ISBN 978-0-646-85383-3 (digital)

www.ingramcontent.com/pod-product-compliance
Lightning Source LLC
Chambersburg PA
CBHW020516120726
47904CB00003B/853